GREEN LANTERN

THE ANIMATED SERIES ™

STONE ARCH BOOKS

a capstone imprint

STONE ARCH BOOKS™
Published in 2013
A Capstone Imprint
1710 Roe Crest Drive
North Mankato, MN 56003
www.capstonepub.com

DC Comics
1700 Broadway, New York, NY 10019
A Warner Bros. Entertainment Company

Cataloging-in-Publication Data is available at the Library of Congress website:
ISBN: 978-1-4342-4835-0 (library binding)

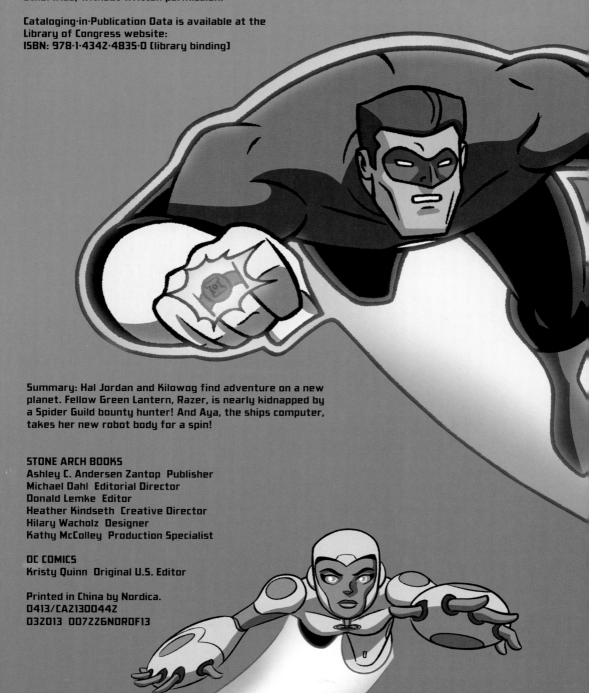

Summary: Hal Jordan and Kilowog find adventure on a new planet. Fellow Green Lantern, Razer, is nearly kidnapped by a Spider Guild bounty hunter! And Aya, the ships computer, takes her new robot body for a spin!

STONE ARCH BOOKS
Ashley C. Andersen Zantop Publisher
Michael Dahl Editorial Director
Donald Lemke Editor
Heather Kindseth Creative Director
Hilary Wacholz Designer
Kathy McColley Production Specialist

DC COMICS
Kristy Quinn Original U.S. Editor

Printed in China by Nordica.
0413/CA21300442
032013 007226NORDF13

GREEN LANTERN

THE ANIMATED SERIES™

BOUNTY HUNTER

Art Baltazar & Franco....................writers
Dario Brizuela............................. illustrator
Gabe Eltaeb & Dario Brizuela.....colorists
Saida Abbott ....letterer

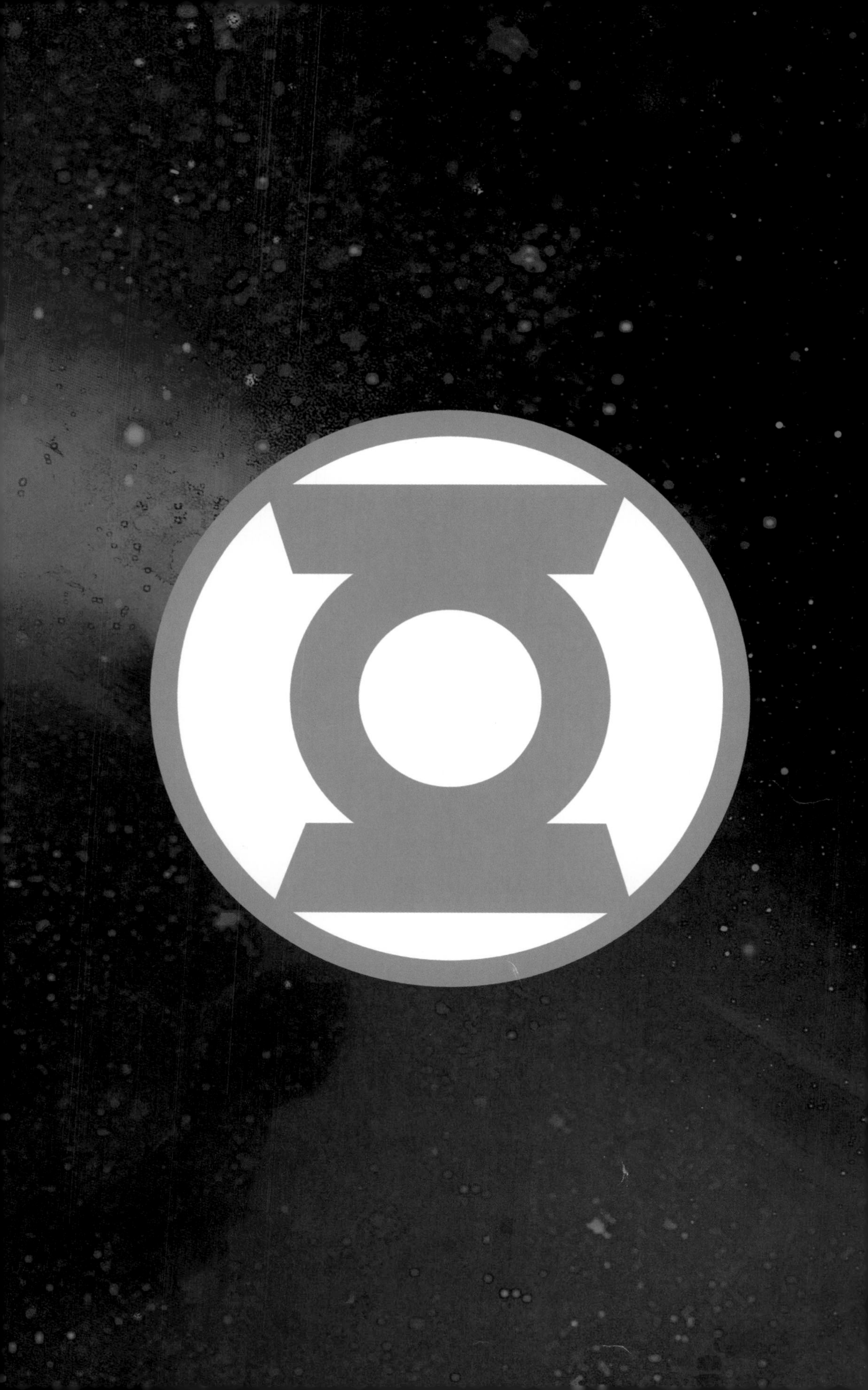

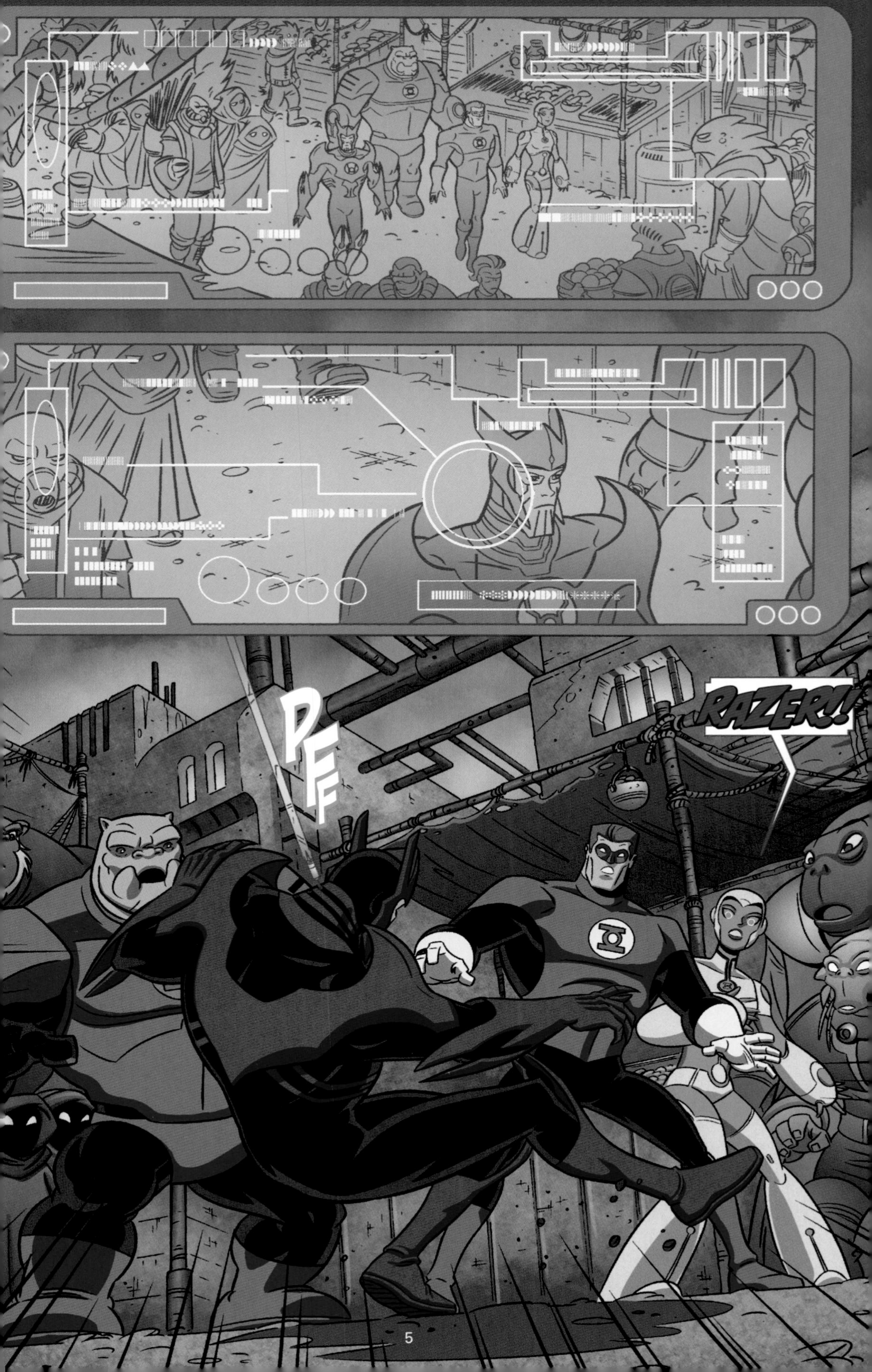
PFF
RAZER!!

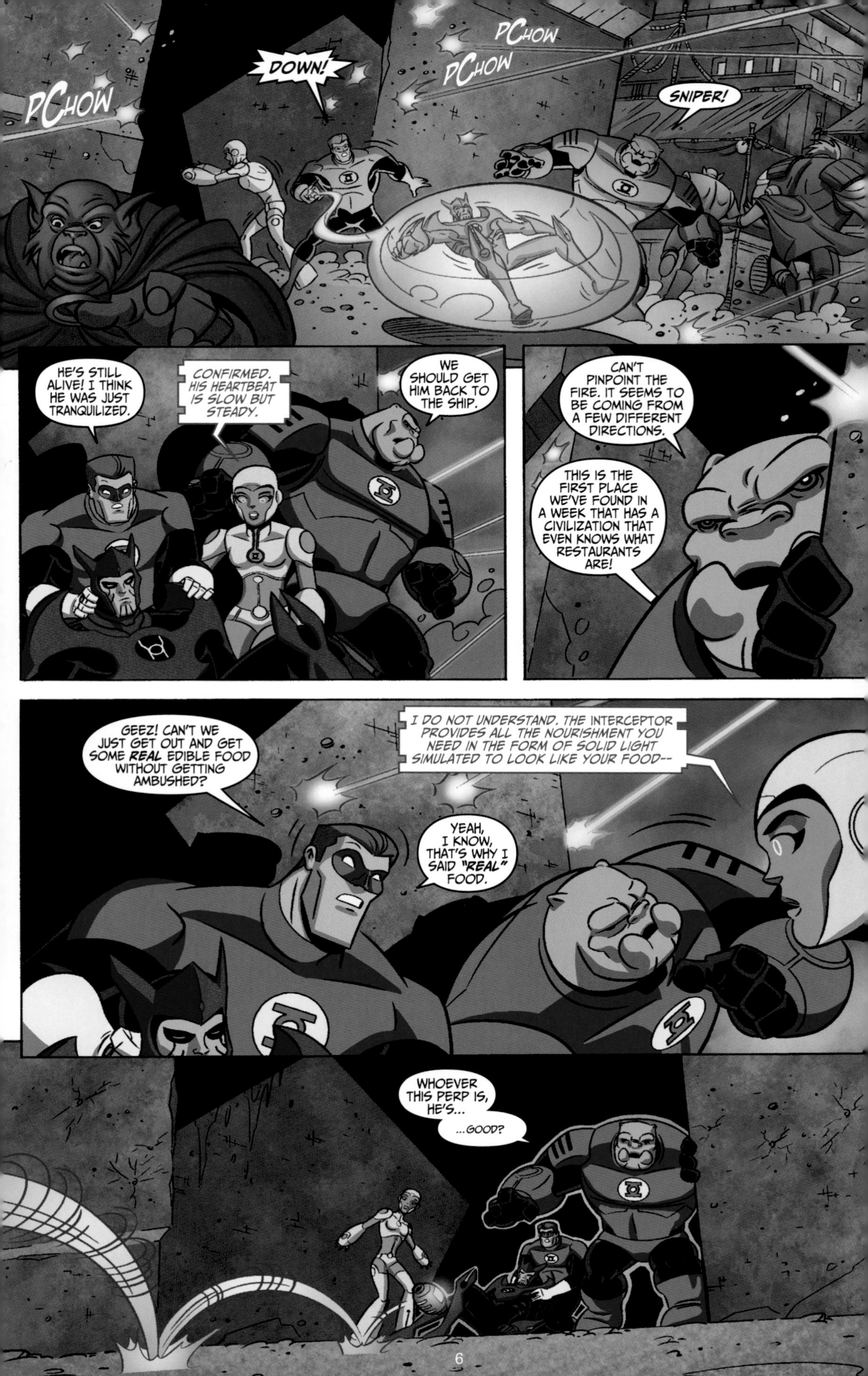
PCHOW
DOWN!
PCHOW
PCHOW
SNIPER!
HE'S STILL ALIVE! I THINK HE WAS JUST TRANQUILIZED.
CONFIRMED. HIS HEARTBEAT IS SLOW BUT STEADY.
WE SHOULD GET HIM BACK TO THE SHIP.
CAN'T PINPOINT THE FIRE. IT SEEMS TO BE COMING FROM A FEW DIFFERENT DIRECTIONS.
THIS IS THE FIRST PLACE WE'VE FOUND IN A WEEK THAT HAS A CIVILIZATION THAT EVEN KNOWS WHAT RESTAURANTS ARE!
GEEZ! CAN'T WE JUST GET OUT AND GET SOME REAL EDIBLE FOOD WITHOUT GETTING AMBUSHED?
I DO NOT UNDERSTAND. THE INTERCEPTOR PROVIDES ALL THE NOURISHMENT YOU NEED IN THE FORM OF SOLID LIGHT SIMULATED TO LOOK LIKE YOUR FOOD--
YEAH, I KNOW, THAT'S WHY I SAID "REAL" FOOD.
WHOEVER THIS PERP IS, HE'S...
...GOOD?

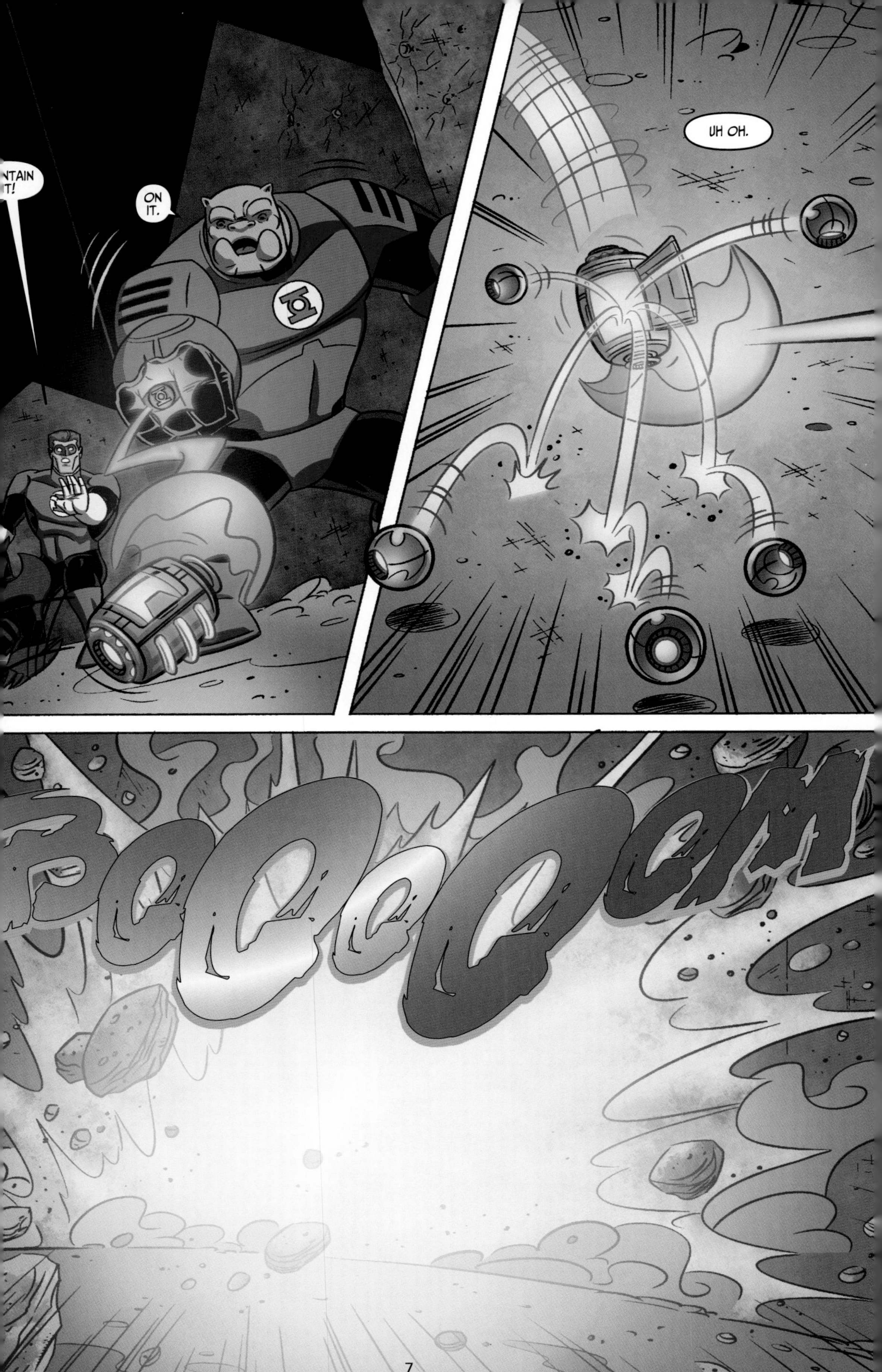
ON IT.
UH OH.
BOOOOOM

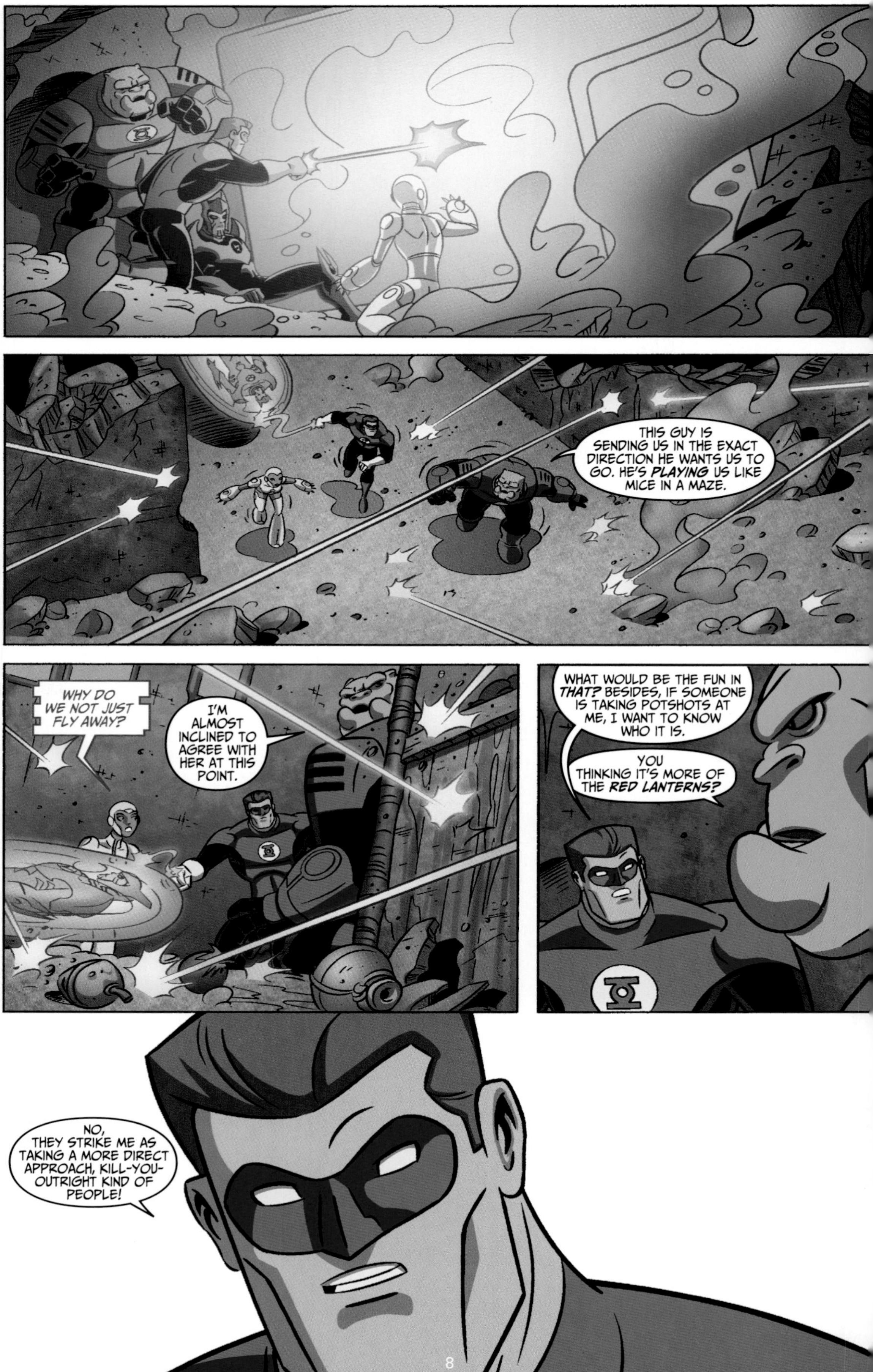

THIS GUY IS SENDING US IN THE EXACT DIRECTION HE WANTS US TO GO. HE'S PLAYING US LIKE MICE IN A MAZE.
WHY DO WE NOT JUST FLY AWAY?
I'M ALMOST INCLINED TO AGREE WITH HER AT THIS POINT.
WHAT WOULD BE THE FUN IN THAT? BESIDES, IF SOMEONE IS TAKING POTSHOTS AT ME, I WANT TO KNOW WHO IT IS.
YOU THINKING IT'S MORE OF THE RED LANTERNS?
NO, THEY STRIKE ME AS TAKING A MORE DIRECT APPROACH, KILL-YOU-OUTRIGHT KIND OF PEOPLE!

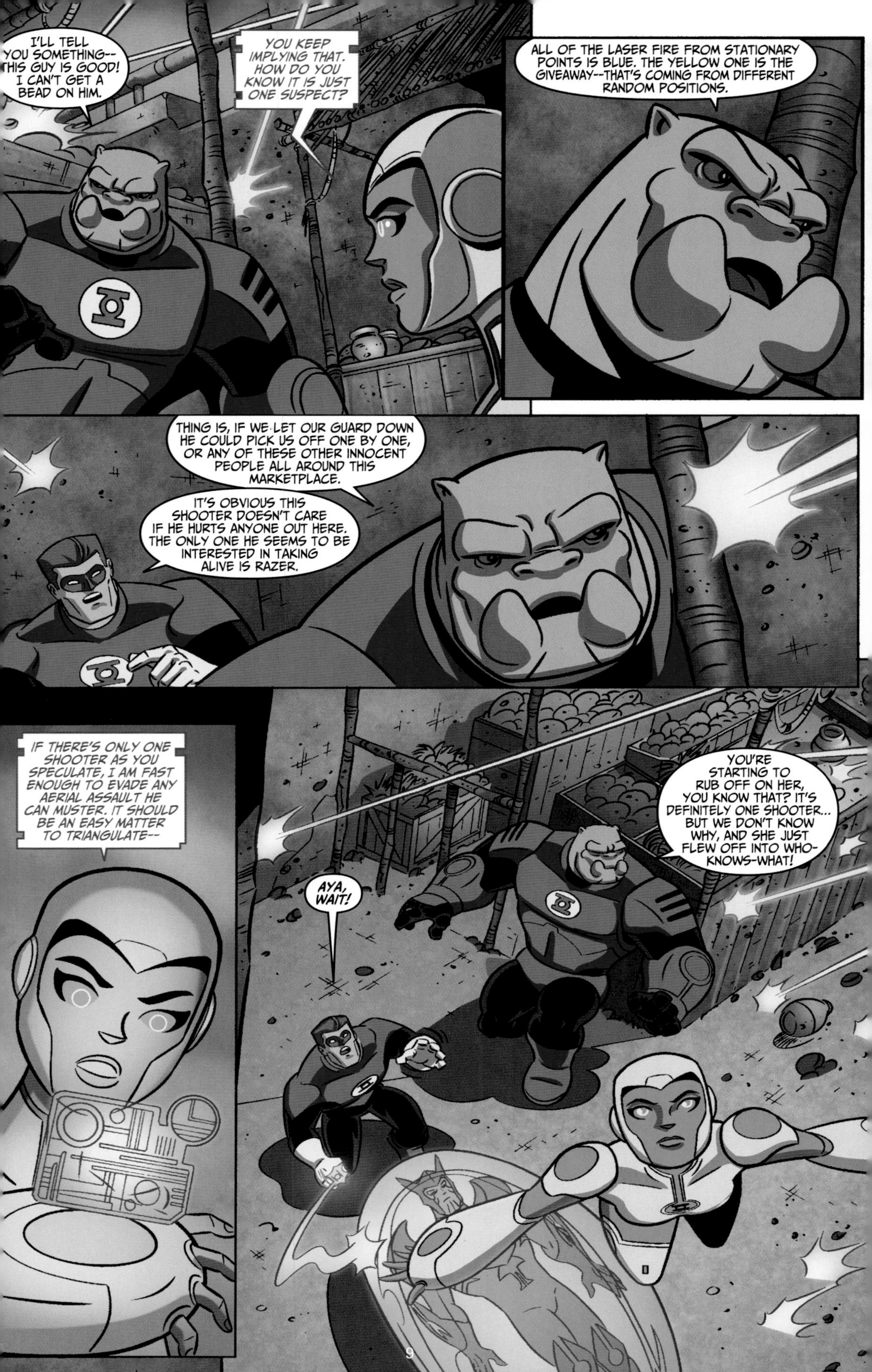
I'LL TELL YOU SOMETHING-- THIS GUY IS GOOD! I CAN'T GET A BEAD ON HIM.
YOU KEEP IMPLYING THAT. HOW DO YOU KNOW IT IS JUST ONE SUSPECT?
ALL OF THE LASER FIRE FROM STATIONARY POINTS IS BLUE. THE YELLOW ONE IS THE GIVEAWAY--THAT'S COMING FROM DIFFERENT RANDOM POSITIONS.
THING IS, IF WE LET OUR GUARD DOWN HE COULD PICK US OFF ONE BY ONE, OR ANY OF THESE OTHER INNOCENT PEOPLE ALL AROUND THIS MARKETPLACE.
IT'S OBVIOUS THIS SHOOTER DOESN'T CARE IF HE HURTS ANYONE OUT HERE. THE ONLY ONE HE SEEMS TO BE INTERESTED IN TAKING ALIVE IS RAZER.
IF THERE'S ONLY ONE SHOOTER AS YOU SPECULATE, I AM FAST ENOUGH TO EVADE ANY AERIAL ASSAULT HE CAN MUSTER. IT SHOULD BE AN EASY MATTER TO TRIANGULATE--
AYA, WAIT!
YOU'RE STARTING TO RUB OFF ON HER, YOU KNOW THAT? IT'S DEFINITELY ONE SHOOTER... BUT WE DON'T KNOW WHY, AND SHE JUST FLEW OFF INTO WHO-KNOWS-WHAT!

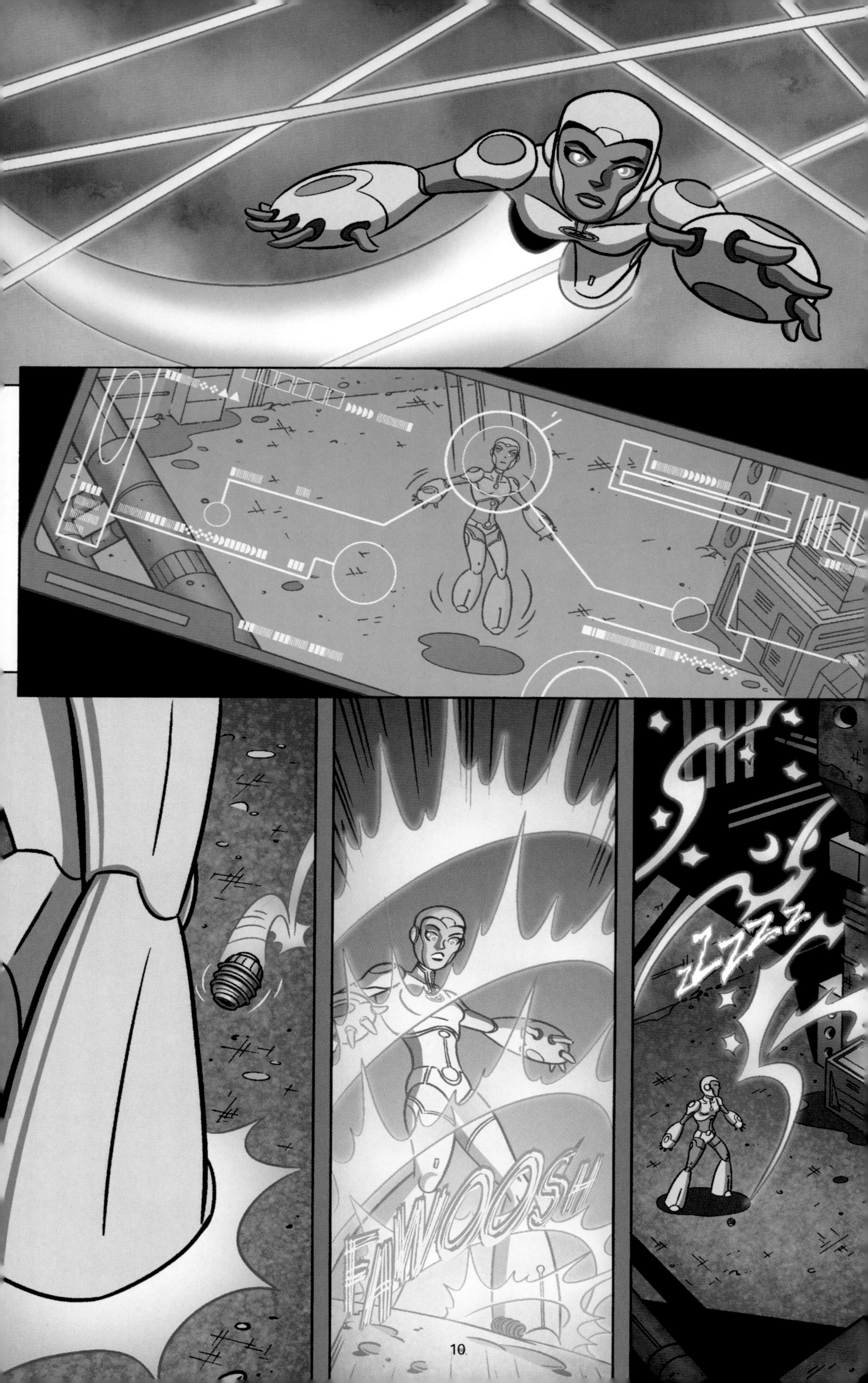
FWOOSH
ZZZZZ

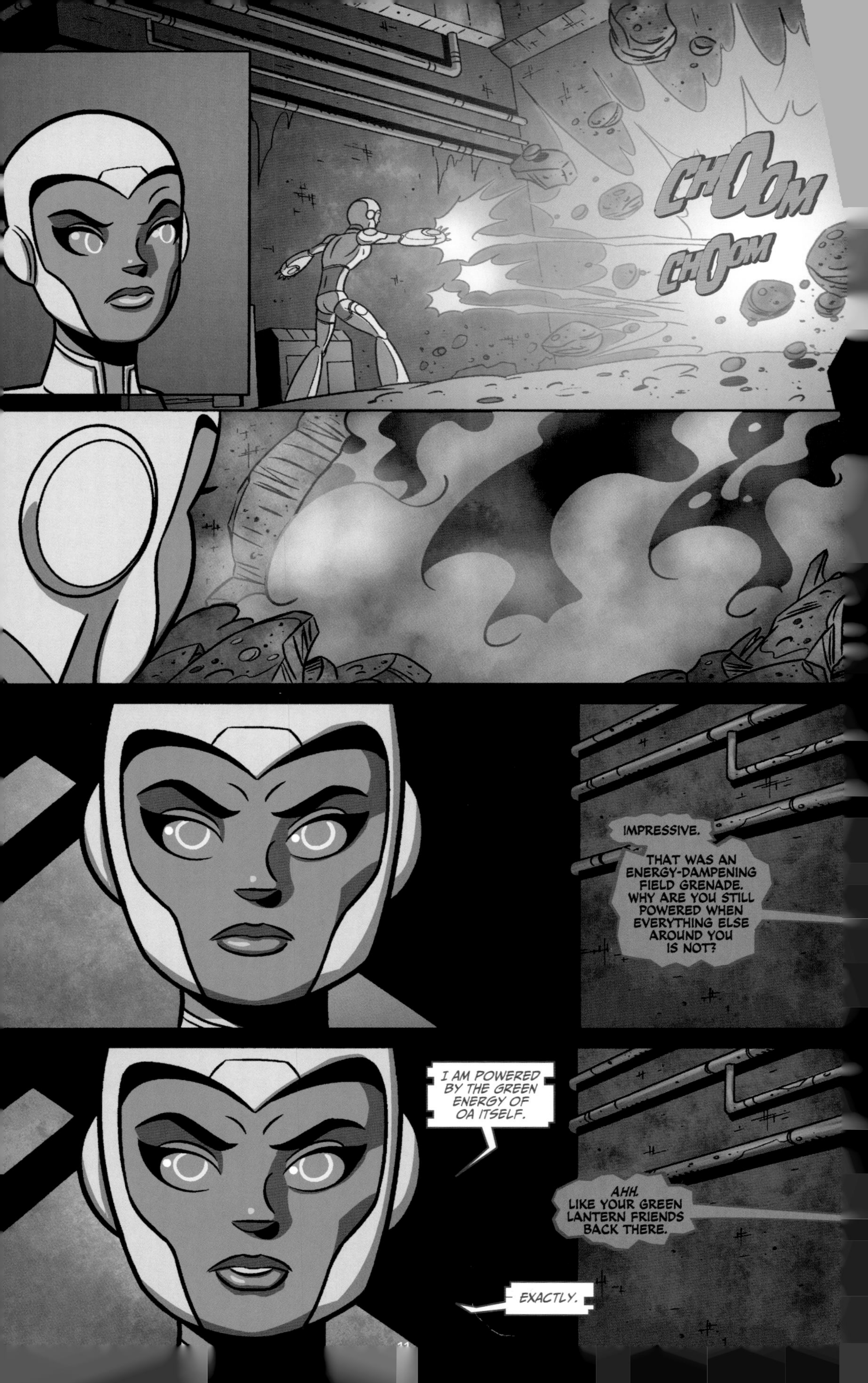
CHOOM
CHOOM
IMPRESSIVE.
THAT WAS AN ENERGY-DAMPENING FIELD GRENADE. WHY ARE YOU STILL POWERED WHEN EVERYTHING ELSE AROUND YOU IS NOT?
I AM POWERED BY THE GREEN ENERGY OF OA ITSELF.
AHH. LIKE YOUR GREEN LANTERN FRIENDS BACK THERE.
EXACTLY.

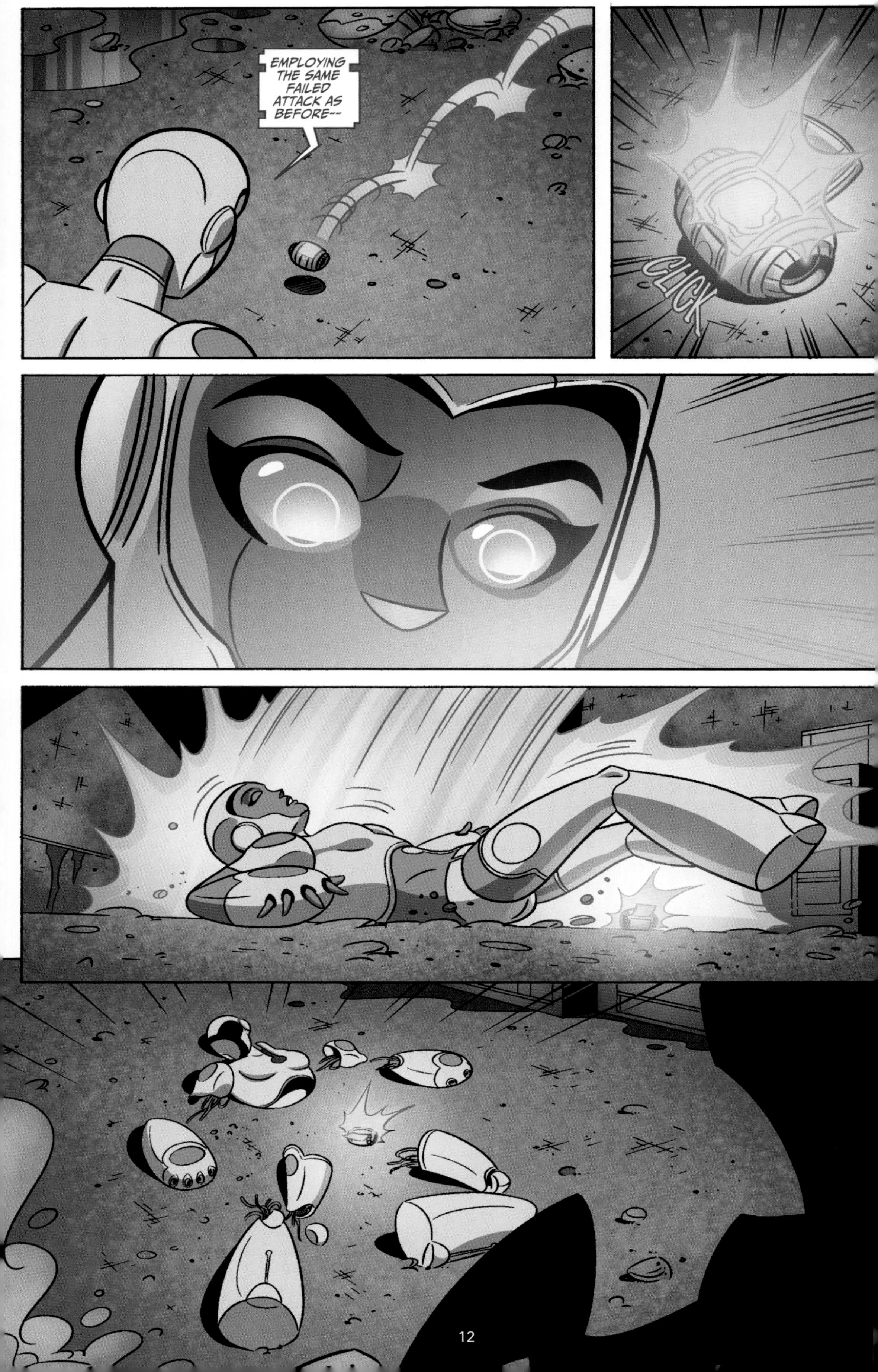
EMPLOYING THE SAME FAILED ATTACK AS BEFORE--
CLICK

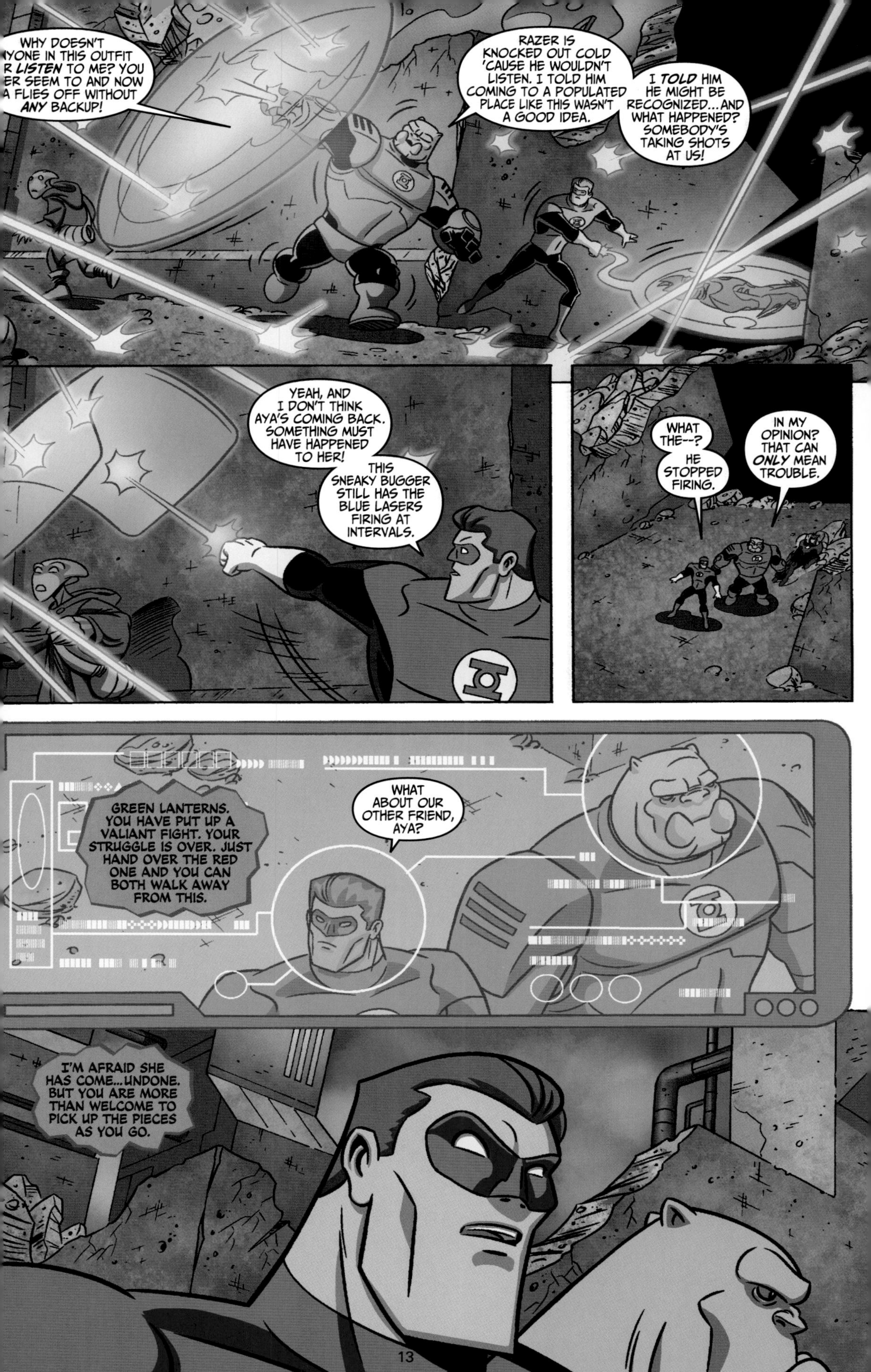
WHY DOESN'T
NYONE IN THIS OUTFIT
R LISTEN TO ME? YOU
ER SEEM TO AND NOW
A FLIES OFF WITHOUT
ANY BACKUP!
RAZER IS KNOCKED OUT COLD 'CAUSE HE WOULDN'T LISTEN. I TOLD HIM COMING TO A POPULATED PLACE LIKE THIS WASN'T A GOOD IDEA.
I TOLD HIM HE MIGHT BE RECOGNIZED...AND WHAT HAPPENED? SOMEBODY'S TAKING SHOTS AT US!
YEAH, AND I DON'T THINK AYA'S COMING BACK. SOMETHING MUST HAVE HAPPENED TO HER!
THIS SNEAKY BUGGER STILL HAS THE BLUE LASERS FIRING AT INTERVALS.
WHAT THE--?
HE STOPPED FIRING.
IN MY OPINION? THAT CAN ONLY MEAN TROUBLE.
GREEN LANTERNS. YOU HAVE PUT UP A VALIANT FIGHT. YOUR STRUGGLE IS OVER. JUST HAND OVER THE RED ONE AND YOU CAN BOTH WALK AWAY FROM THIS.
WHAT ABOUT OUR OTHER FRIEND, AYA?
I'M AFRAID SHE HAS COME...UNDONE. BUT YOU ARE MORE THAN WELCOME TO PICK UP THE PIECES AS YOU GO.

HE MUST HAVE KNOWN WE'D END UP HERE AT SOME POINT. IT'S THE ONLY REAL MARKET IN THIS SECTOR.

HE'S BEEN PLANNING THIS AMBUSH FOR WEEKS.

IF IT WAS A TEAM, THEY COULD HAVE COME AFTER THE SHIP--ONLY A GUY WORKING ALONE WOULD GO TO SO MUCH TROUBLE TO TAKE RAZER *ALIVE.*

YEAH, WE CAN ALL AGREE, HE DEFINITELY SAW US COMING. YOUR *POINT* BEING?

HE'S GOT ALL THE ANGLES COVERED, PUTTING INNOCENT LIVES IN DANGER SO WE'LL STAY AND PROTECT THEM. IF THE TWO OF US ABANDONED RAZER AND FLEW OFF, HE'D PROBABLY SHOOT US OUT OF THE AIR!

PROBABLY. IT WOULD EXPLAIN WHY AYA HASN'T RETURNED.

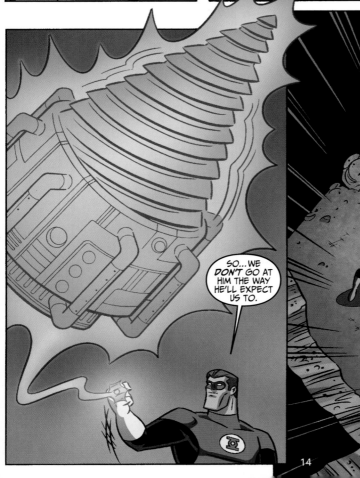

SO...WE *DON'T* GO AT HIM THE WAY HE'LL EXPECT US TO.

GOOD THINKING.

I'M ANNOYED... MAKE SURE YOU SAVE ME SOME *SMACKDOWN* TIME ON THIS CREEP!

14

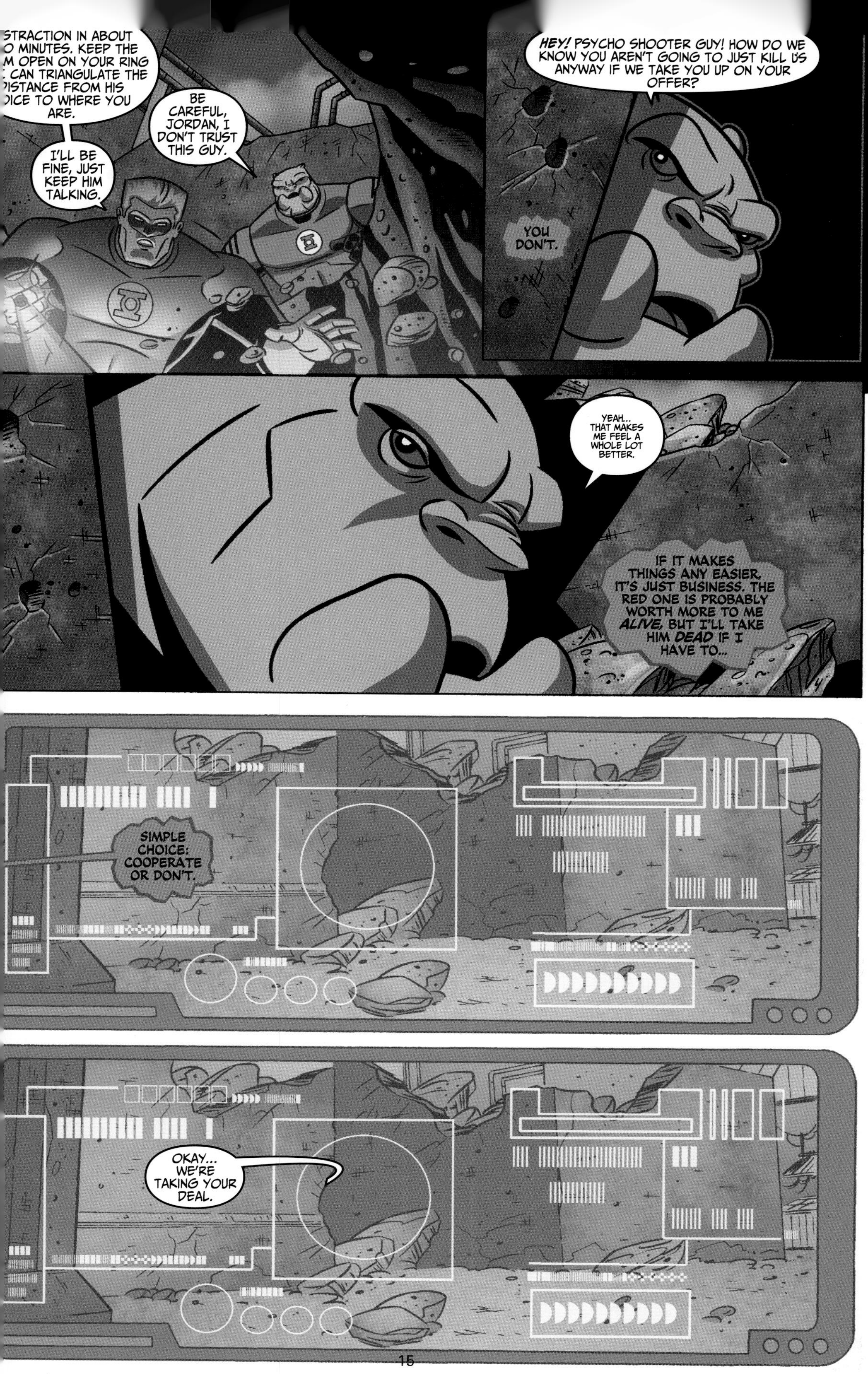
STRACTION IN ABOUT
O MINUTES. KEEP THE
M OPEN ON YOUR RING
CAN TRIANGULATE THE
DISTANCE FROM HIS
OICE TO WHERE YOU
ARE.
I'LL BE FINE, JUST KEEP HIM TALKING.
BE CAREFUL, JORDAN, I DON'T TRUST THIS GUY.
HEY! PSYCHO SHOOTER GUY! HOW DO WE KNOW YOU AREN'T GOING TO JUST KILL US ANYWAY IF WE TAKE YOU UP ON YOUR OFFER?
YOU DON'T.
YEAH... THAT MAKES ME FEEL A WHOLE LOT BETTER.
IF IT MAKES THINGS ANY EASIER, IT'S JUST BUSINESS. THE RED ONE IS PROBABLY WORTH MORE TO ME ALIVE, BUT I'LL TAKE HIM DEAD IF I HAVE TO...
SIMPLE CHOICE: COOPERATE OR DON'T.
OKAY... WE'RE TAKING YOUR DEAL.

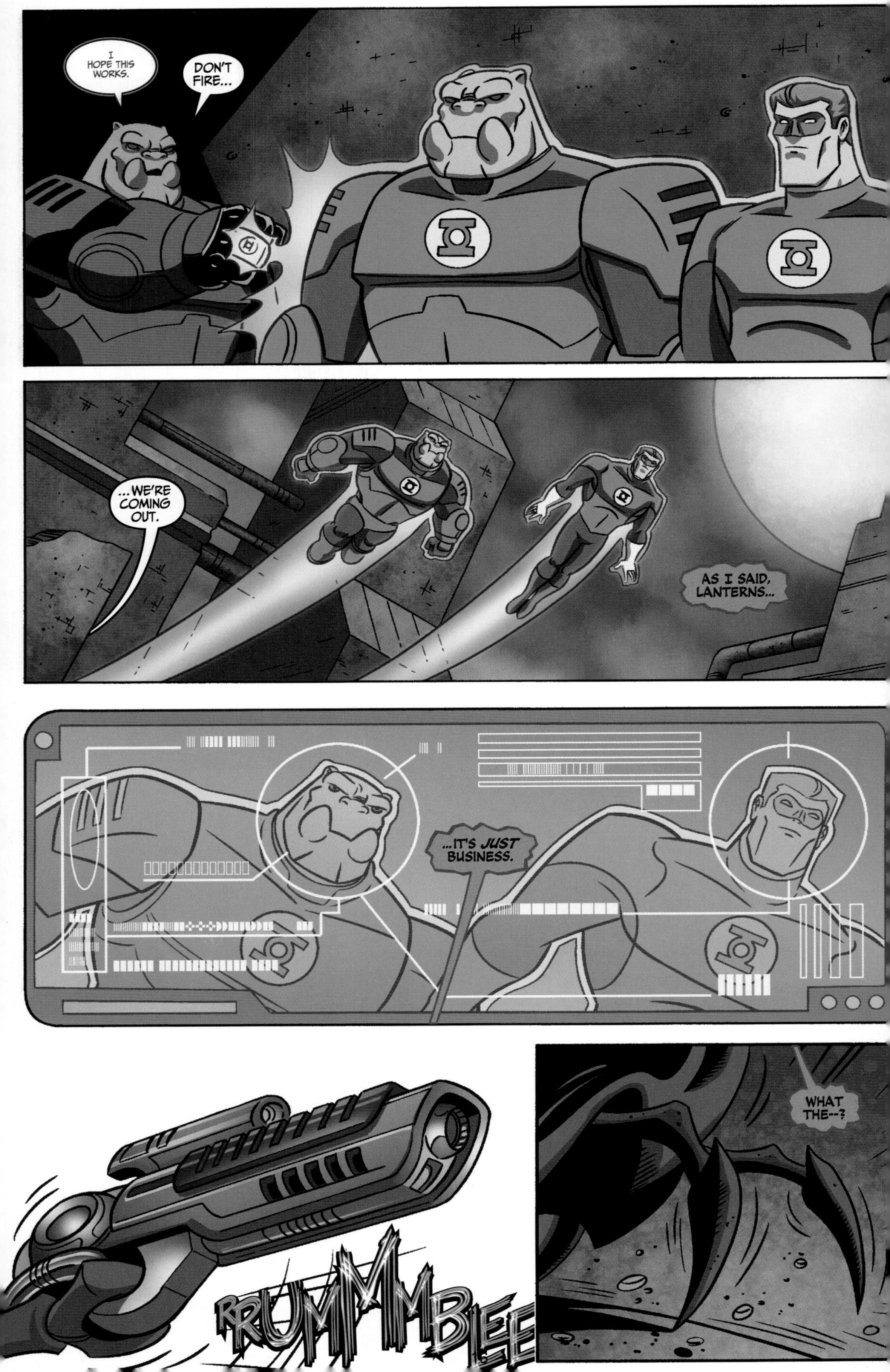

I HOPE THIS WORKS.
DON'T FIRE...
...WE'RE COMING OUT.
AS I SAID, LANTERNS...
...IT'S JUST BUSINESS.
RRUMMMBLEE
WHAT THE--?

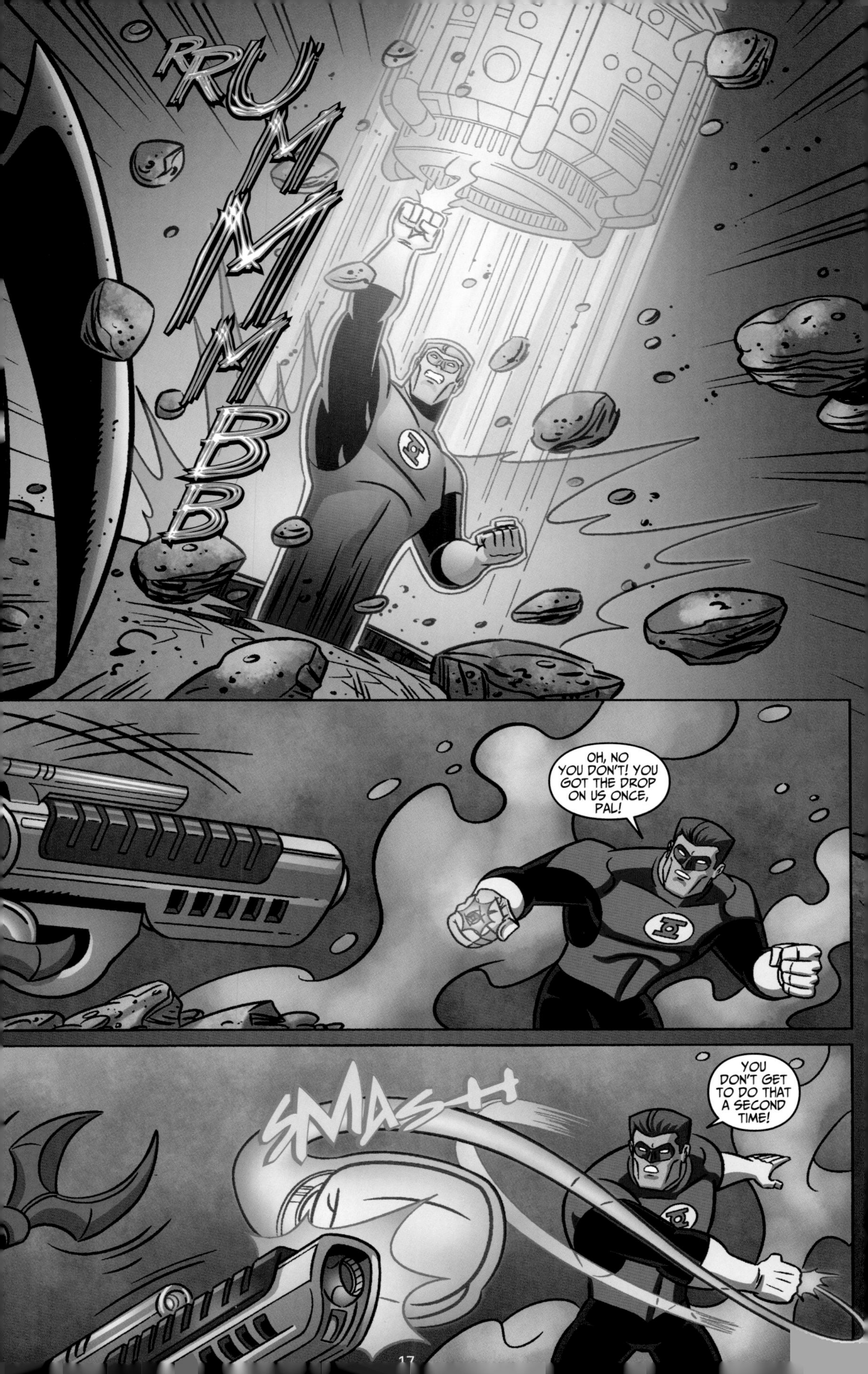
RRUMMMBBB
OH, NO YOU DON'T! YOU GOT THE DROP ON US ONCE, PAL!
SMASH
YOU DON'T GET TO DO THAT A SECOND TIME!

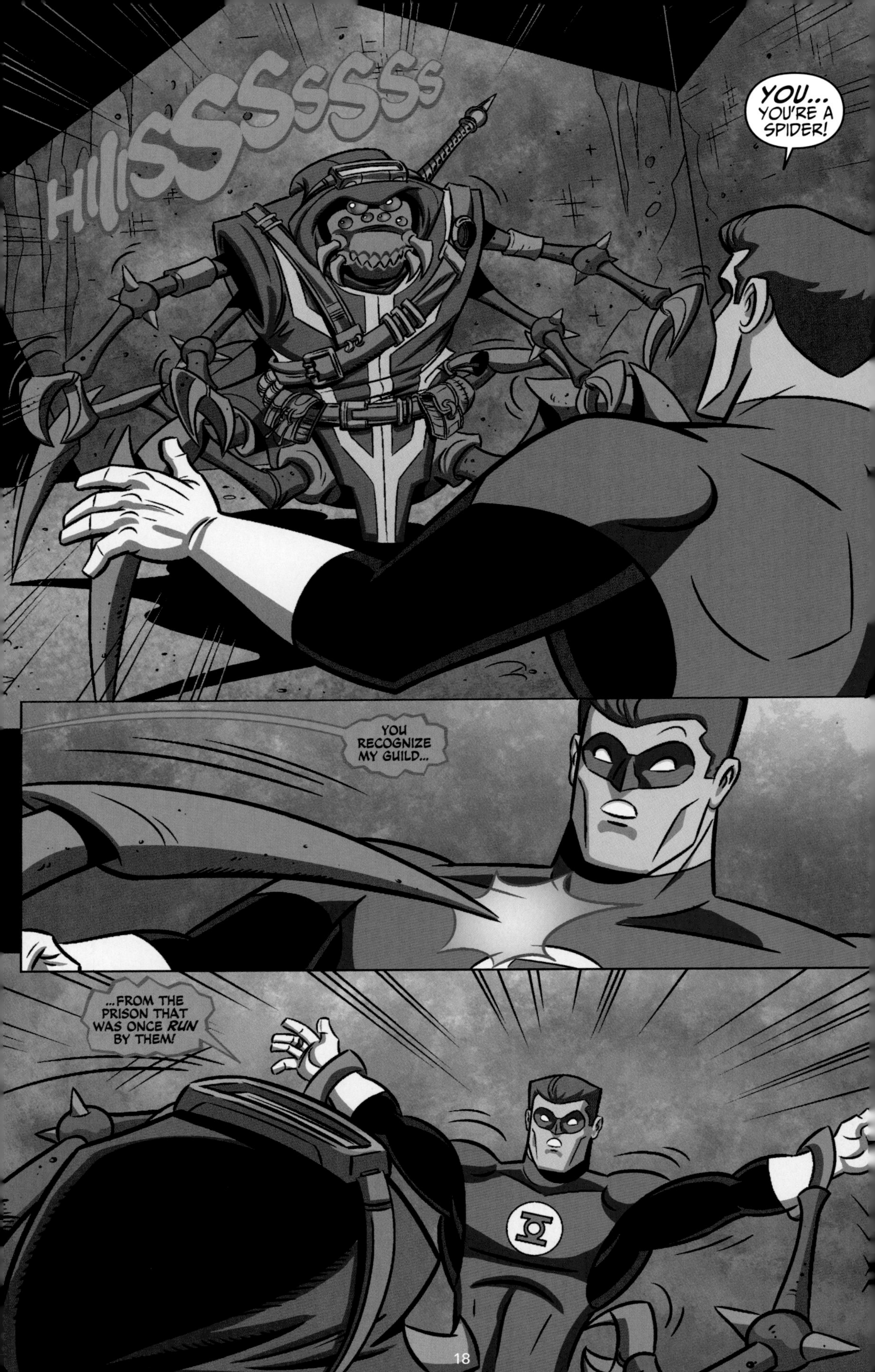
HIIISSSSSSS
YOU... YOU'RE A SPIDER!
YOU RECOGNIZE MY GUILD...
...FROM THE PRISON THAT WAS ONCE *RUN* BY THEM!

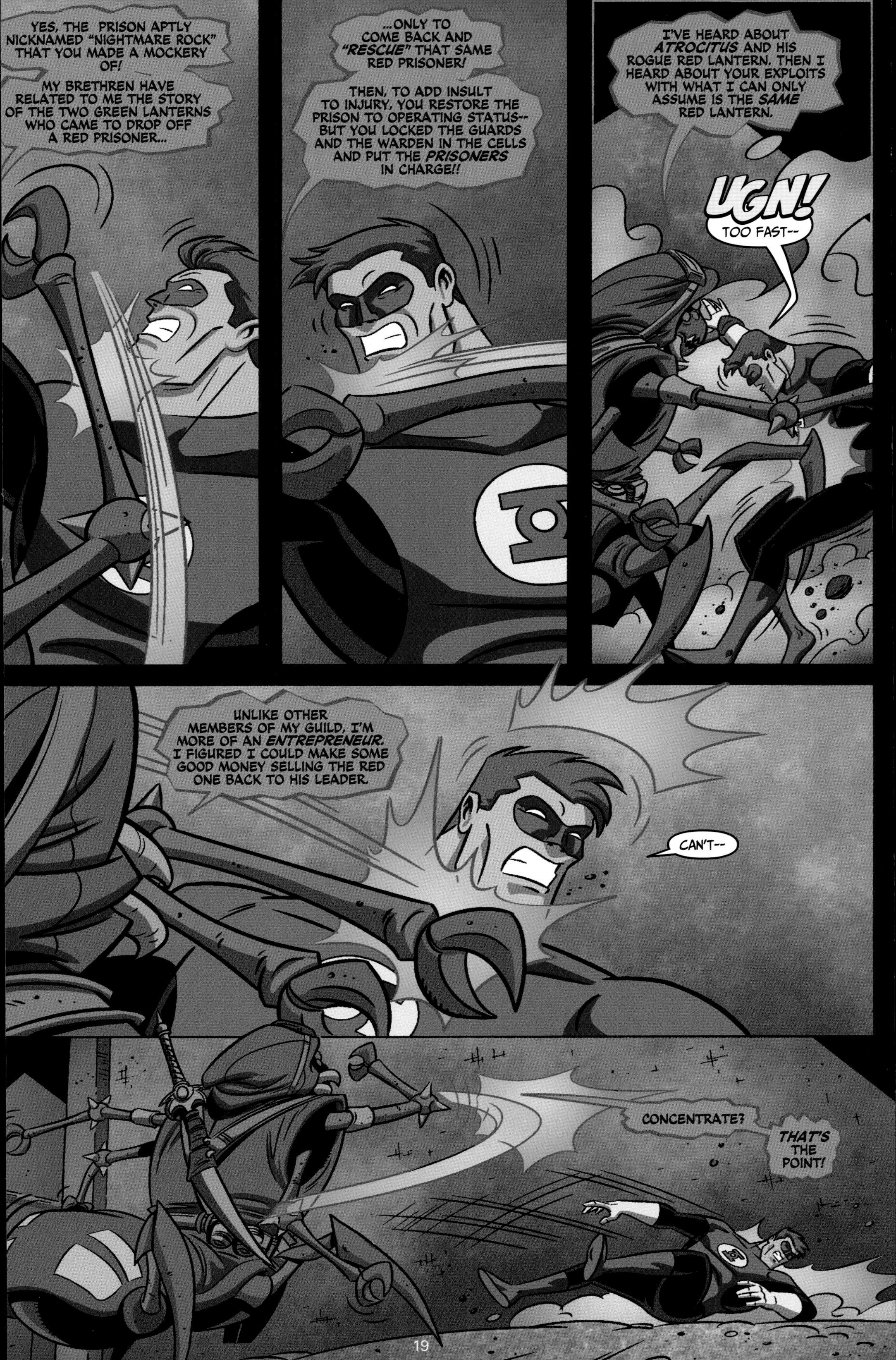
YES, THE PRISON APTLY NICKNAMED "NIGHTMARE ROCK" THAT YOU MADE A MOCKERY OF!
MY BRETHREN HAVE RELATED TO ME THE STORY OF THE TWO GREEN LANTERNS WHO CAME TO DROP OFF A RED PRISONER...
...ONLY TO COME BACK AND "RESCUE" THAT SAME RED PRISONER!
THEN, TO ADD INSULT TO INJURY, YOU RESTORE THE PRISON TO OPERATING STATUS-- BUT YOU LOCKED THE GUARDS AND THE WARDEN IN THE CELLS AND PUT THE PRISONERS IN CHARGE!!
I'VE HEARD ABOUT ATROCITUS AND HIS ROGUE RED LANTERN. THEN I HEARD ABOUT YOUR EXPLOITS WITH WHAT I CAN ONLY ASSUME IS THE SAME RED LANTERN.
UGN!
TOO FAST--
UNLIKE OTHER MEMBERS OF MY GUILD, I'M MORE OF AN ENTREPRENEUR. I FIGURED I COULD MAKE SOME GOOD MONEY SELLING THE RED ONE BACK TO HIS LEADER.
CAN'T--
CONCENTRATE?
THAT'S THE POINT!

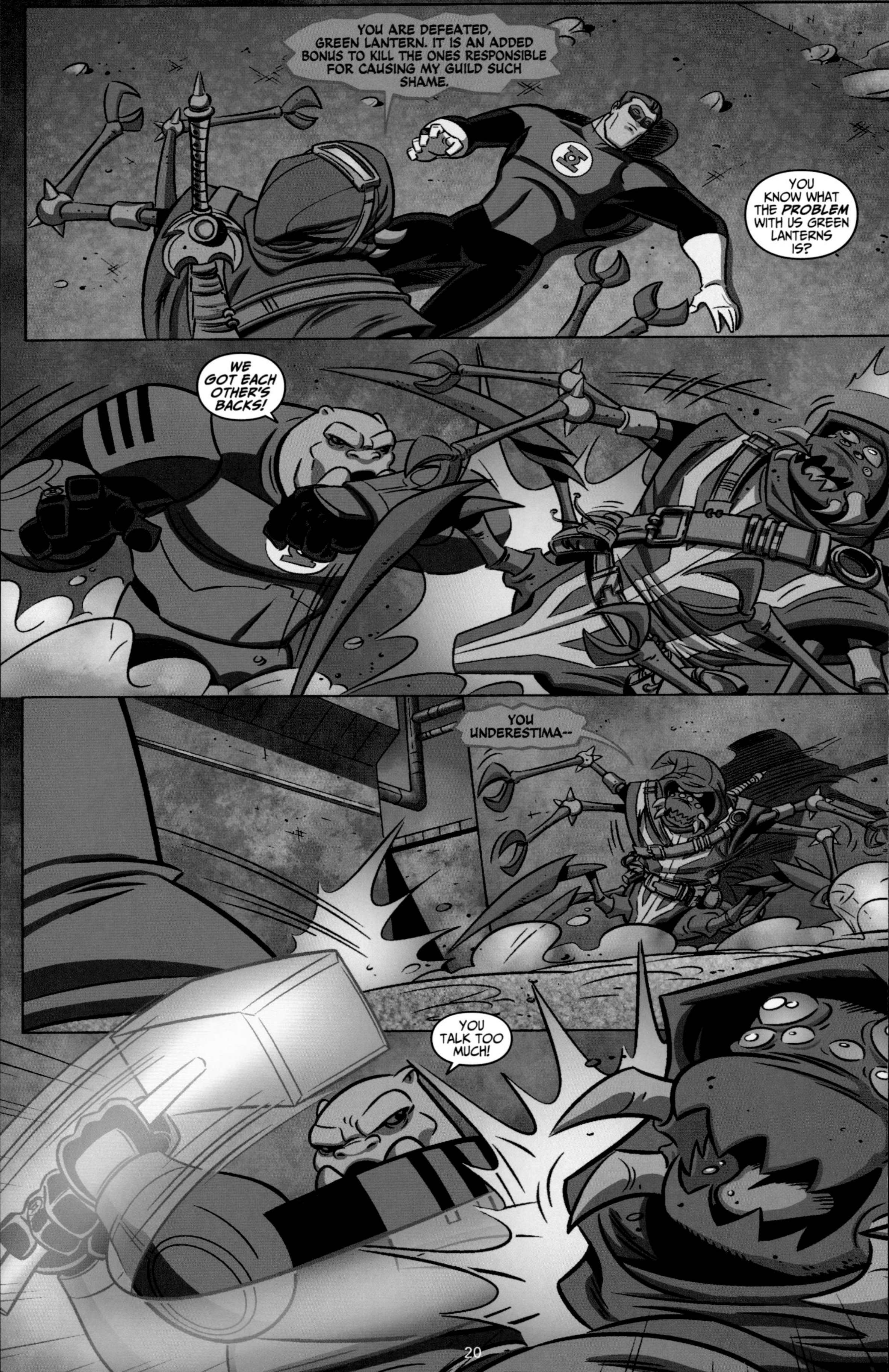
YOU ARE DEFEATED, GREEN LANTERN. IT IS AN ADDED BONUS TO KILL THE ONES RESPONSIBLE FOR CAUSING MY GUILD SUCH SHAME.
YOU KNOW WHAT THE PROBLEM WITH US GREEN LANTERNS IS?
WE GOT EACH OTHER'S BACKS!
YOU UNDERESTIMA--
YOU TALK TOO MUCH!

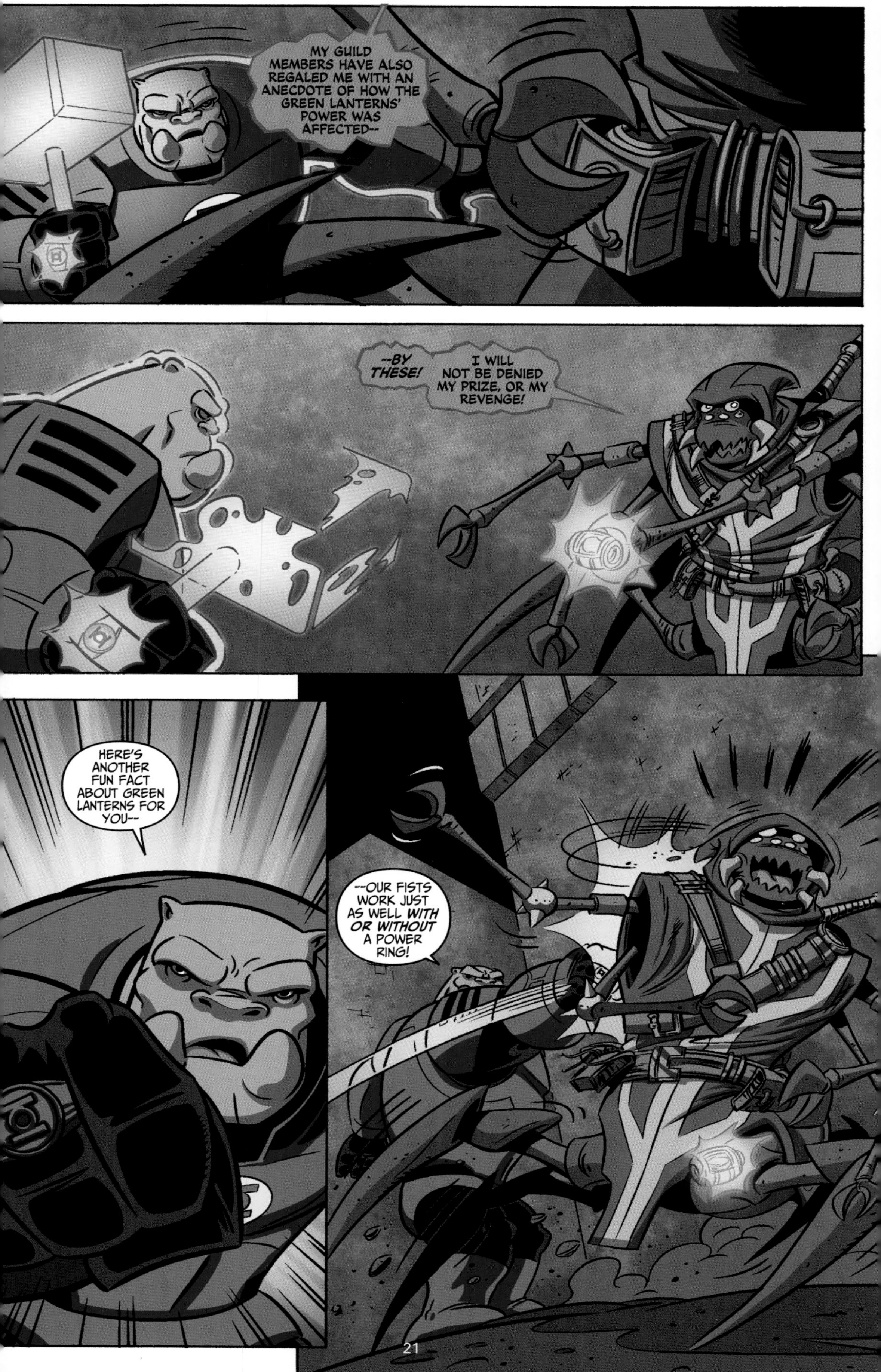
MY GUILD MEMBERS HAVE ALSO REGALED ME WITH AN ANECDOTE OF HOW THE GREEN LANTERNS' POWER WAS AFFECTED--
--BY THESE!
I WILL NOT BE DENIED MY PRIZE, OR MY REVENGE!
HERE'S ANOTHER FUN FACT ABOUT GREEN LANTERNS FOR YOU--
--OUR FISTS WORK JUST AS WELL WITH OR WITHOUT A POWER RING!

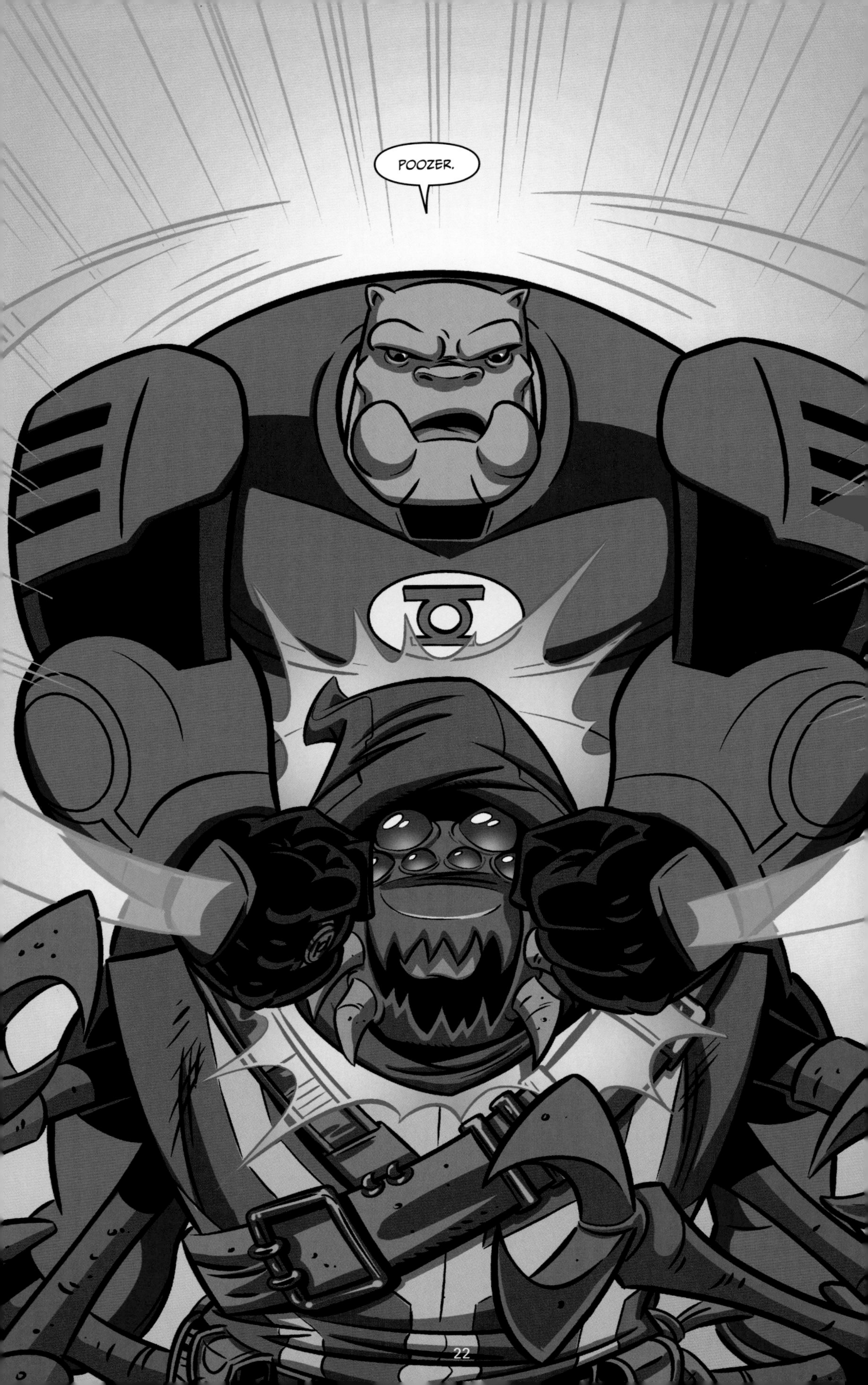
POOZER.

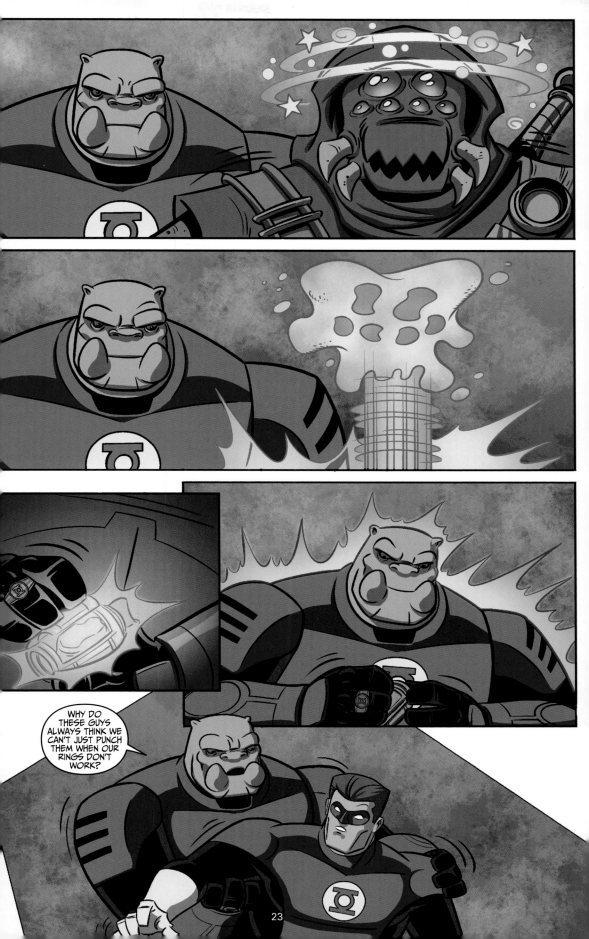

WHY DO THESE GUYS ALWAYS THINK WE CAN'T JUST PUNCH THEM WHEN OUR RINGS DON'T WORK?

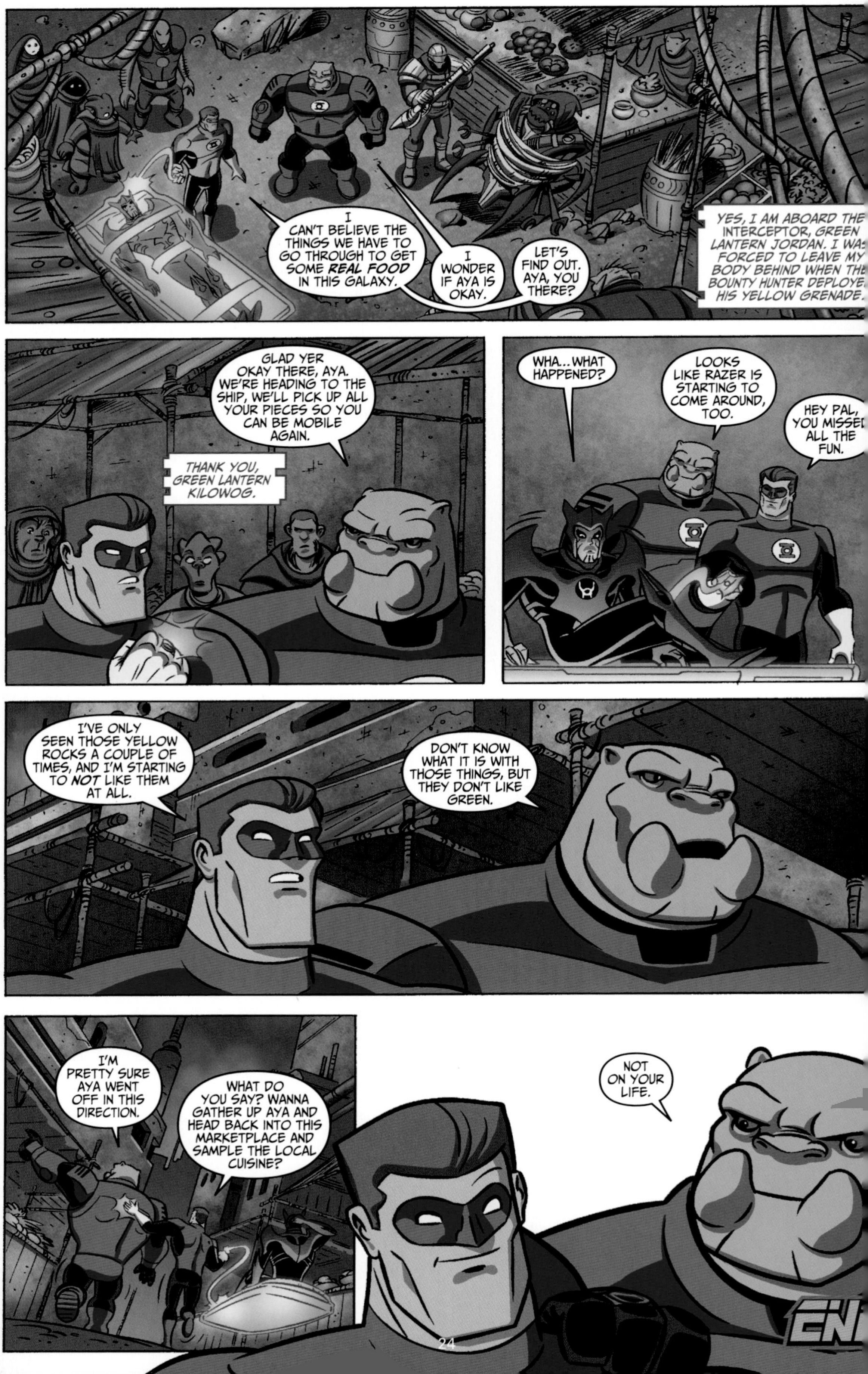
I CAN'T BELIEVE THE THINGS WE HAVE TO GO THROUGH TO GET SOME **REAL FOOD** IN THIS GALAXY.
I WONDER IF AYA IS OKAY.
LET'S FIND OUT. AYA, YOU THERE?
YES, I AM ABOARD THE INTERCEPTOR, GREEN LANTERN JORDAN. I WA FORCED TO LEAVE MY BODY BEHIND WHEN TH BOUNTY HUNTER DEPLOYE HIS YELLOW GRENADE.
GLAD YER OKAY THERE, AYA. WE'RE HEADING TO THE SHIP, WE'LL PICK UP ALL YOUR PIECES SO YOU CAN BE MOBILE AGAIN.
THANK YOU, GREEN LANTERN KILOWOG.
WHA...WHAT HAPPENED?
LOOKS LIKE RAZER IS STARTING TO COME AROUND, TOO.
HEY PAL, YOU MISSE ALL THE FUN.
I'VE ONLY SEEN THOSE YELLOW ROCKS A COUPLE OF TIMES, AND I'M STARTING TO **NOT** LIKE THEM AT ALL.
DON'T KNOW WHAT IT IS WITH THOSE THINGS, BUT THEY DON'T LIKE GREEN.
I'M PRETTY SURE AYA WENT OFF IN THIS DIRECTION.
WHAT DO YOU SAY? WANNA GATHER UP AYA AND HEAD BACK INTO THIS MARKETPLACE AND SAMPLE THE LOCAL CUISINE?
NOT ON YOUR LIFE.

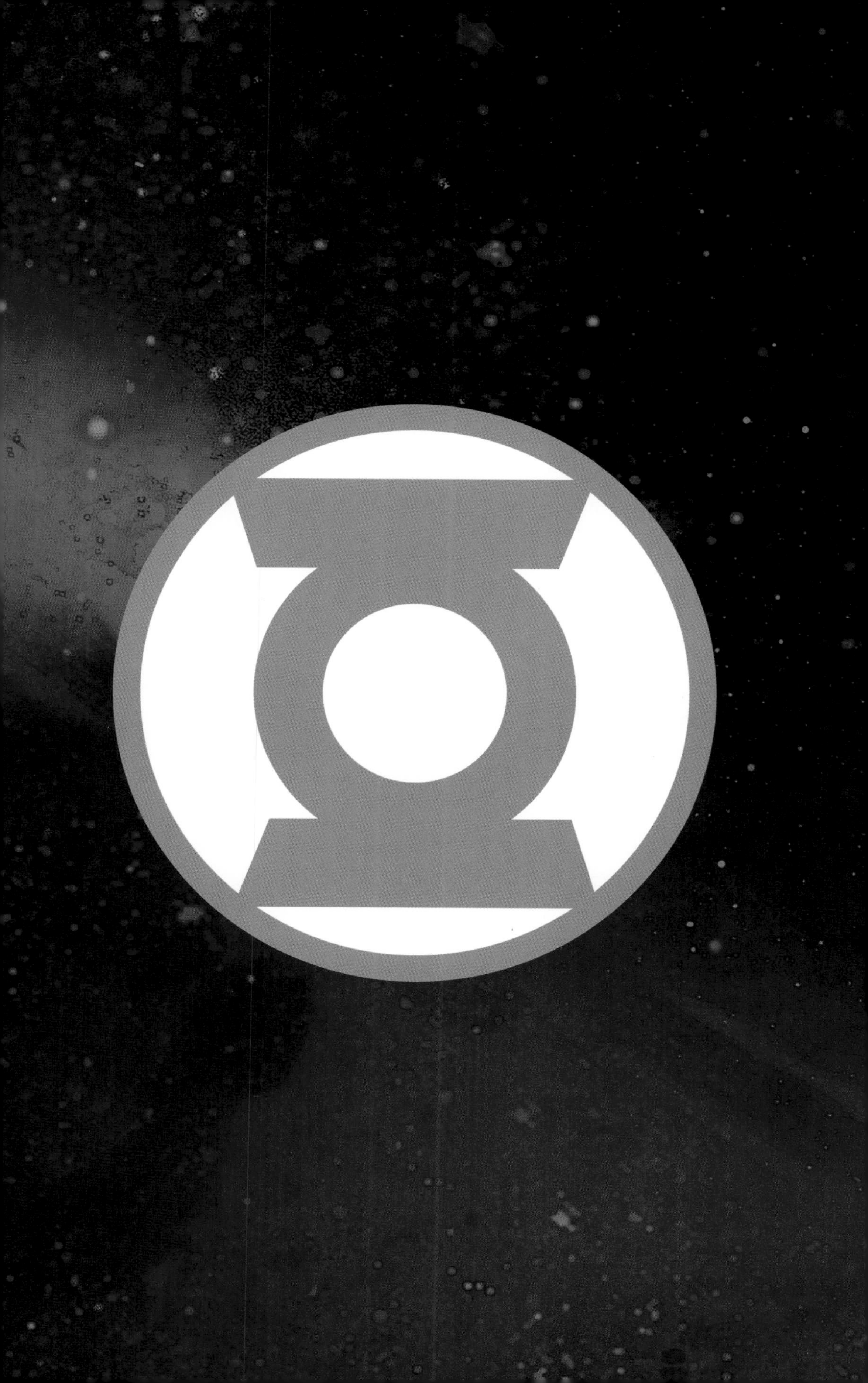

DRAW YOUR OWN GREEN LANTERN AYA!

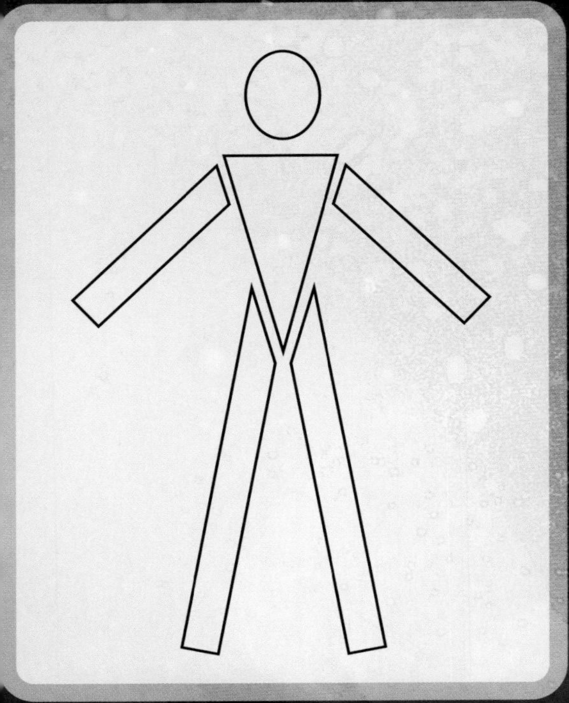

1.) Using a pencil, start with some basic shapes to build a "body."

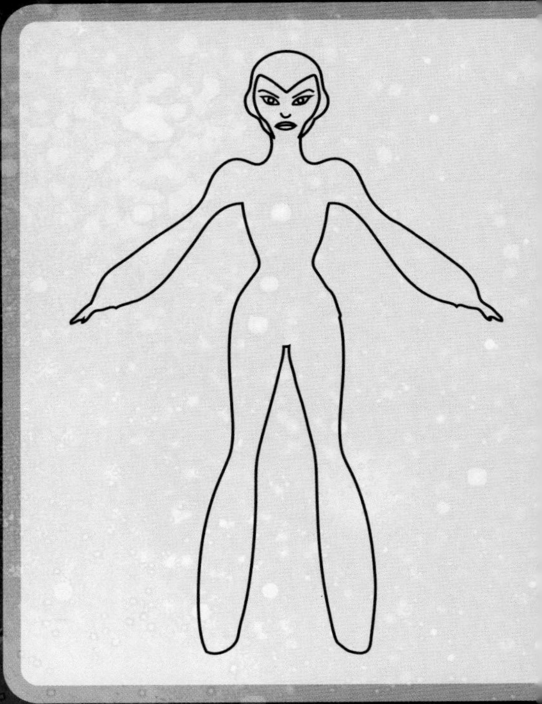

2.) Smooth your outline, and begin adding facial features.

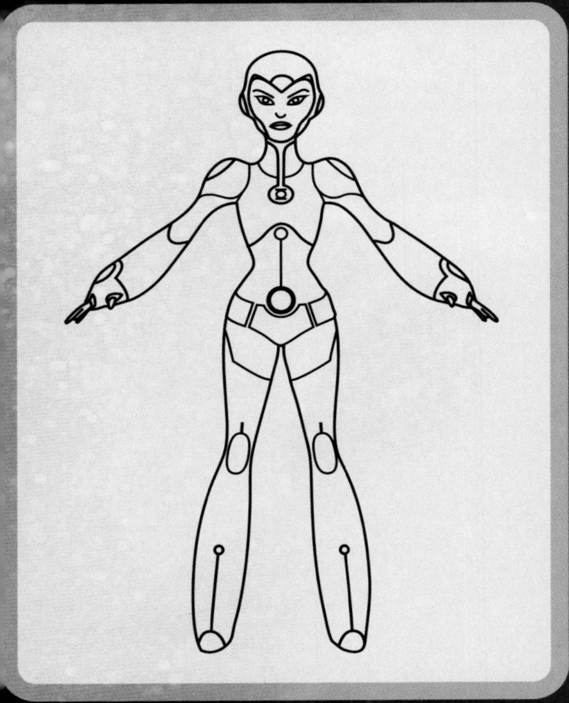

3.) Add in costume details, like Aya's suit, helmet,

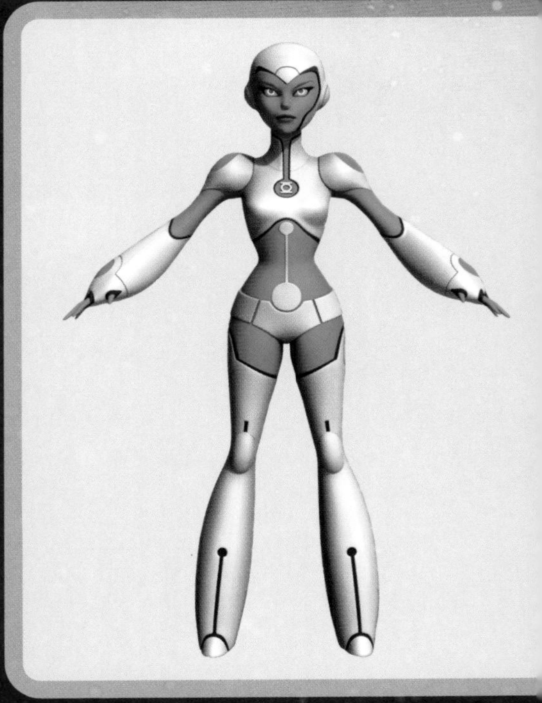

4.) Fill in the colors with crayons or markers.

ART BALTAZAR *writer*

Art Baltazar is a cartoonist machine from the heart of Chicago! He defines cartoons and comics not only as an art style, but as a way of life. Currently, Art is the creative force behind *The New York Times* best-selling, Eisner Award-winning, DC Comics series Tiny Titans, and the co-writer for *Billy Batson and the Magic of SHAZAM!* and co-creator of the Superman Family Adventures series. Art is living the dream! He draws comics and never has to leave the house. He lives with his lovely wife, Rose, big boy Sonny, little boy Gordon, and little girl Audrey. Right on!

FRANCO AURELIANI *writer*

Bronx, New York born writer and artist Franco Aureliani has been drawing comics since he could hold a crayon. Currently residing in upstate New York with his wife, Ivette, and son, Nicolas, Franco spends most of his days in a Batcave-like studio where he produces DC's Tiny Titans comics. In 1995, Franco founded Blindwolf Studios, an independent art studio where he and fellow creators can create children's comics. Franco is the creator, artist, and writer of *Weirdsville*, *L'il Creeps*, and *Eagle All Star*, as well as the co-creator and writer of *Patrick the Wolf Boy*. When he's not writing and drawing, Franco also teaches high school art.

DARIO BRIZUELA *illustrator*

Dario Brizuela is a professional comic book artist. He's illustrated some of today's most popular characters, including Batman, Green Lantern, Teenage Mutant Ninja Turtles, Thor, Iron Man, and Transformers. His best-known works for DC Comics include the series DC Super Friends, Justice League Unlimited, and Batman: The Brave and the Bold.

ambushed (AM-bushd) — unexpectedly attacked by someone

brethren (BREHTH-ren) — a fellow member of a group

civilization (siv-i-luh-ZAY-shuhn) — a highly developed and organized society

edible (ED-uh-buhl) — able to be eaten

entrepreneur (on-truh-pruh-NUR) — one who organizes, manages, and takes on the risks of a business

galaxy (GAL-uhk-see) — a very large group of stars and planets

nourishment (NUR-ish-muhnt) — something that promotes growth or development, such as food

speculate (SPEK-yuh-late) — to wonder or guess about something without knowing all the facts

valiant (VAL-yuhnt) — brave or courageous

VISUAL QUESTIONS

1. Describe what is happening in the panels below, from page 5. Why are the panels green and filled with information? What clues in the story helped you find your answer.

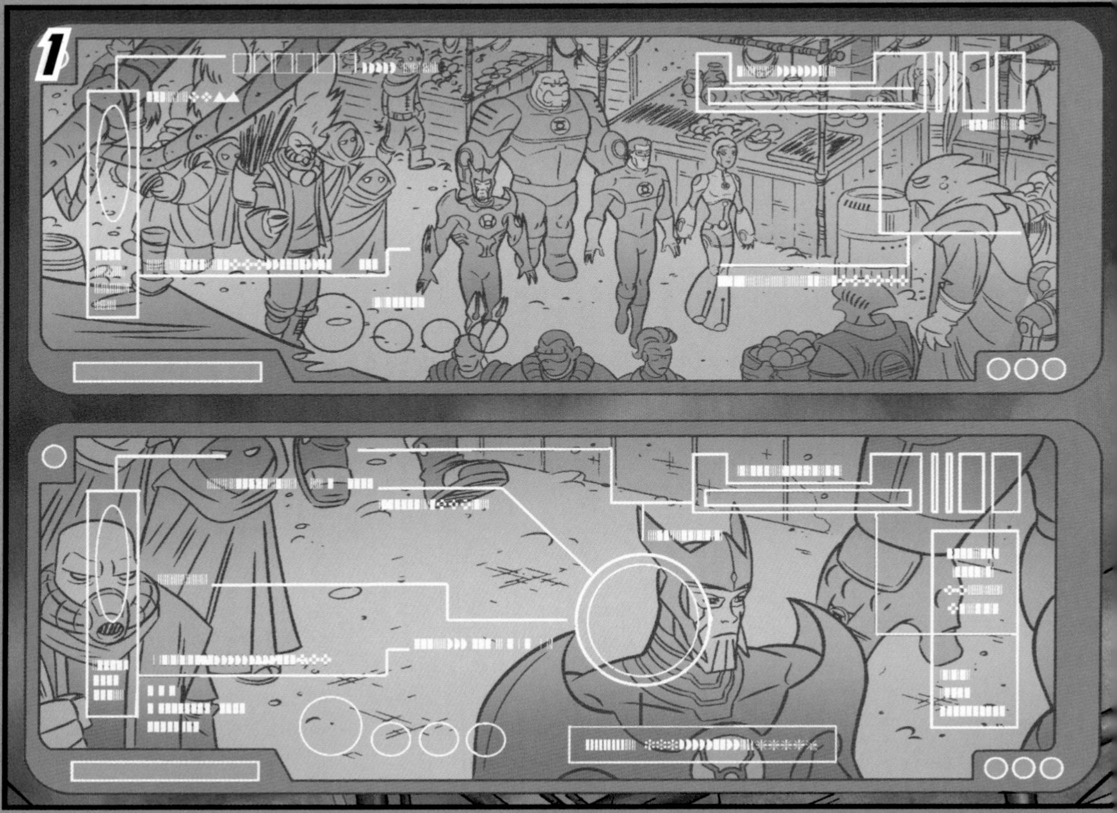

2. Green Lanterns come in all shapes, sizes, and species. Create your own Green Lantern Corp Member. Where does it come from? What does it look like? Write a description of your Green Lantern, and then draw a picture of it.

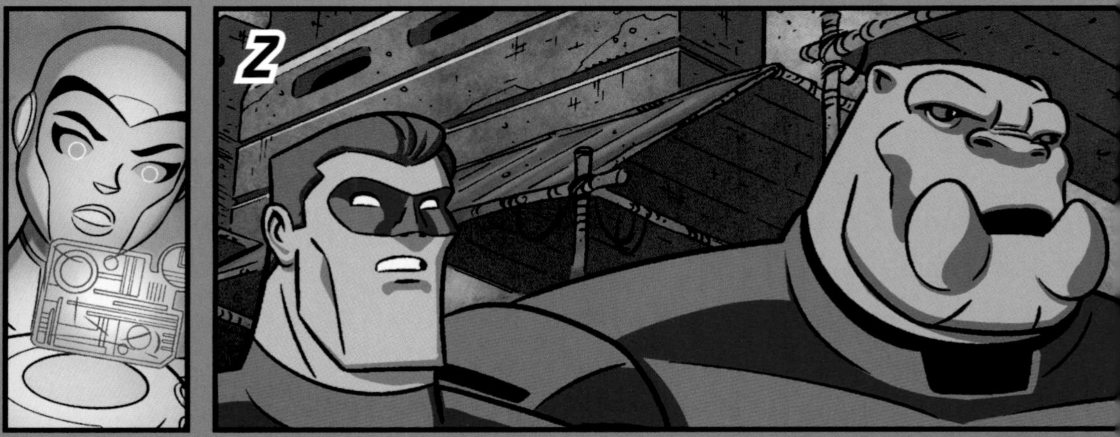

3. With his powerful green ring, Hal Jordan can create anything he imagines. If you wore a power ring, what would you create? Why?

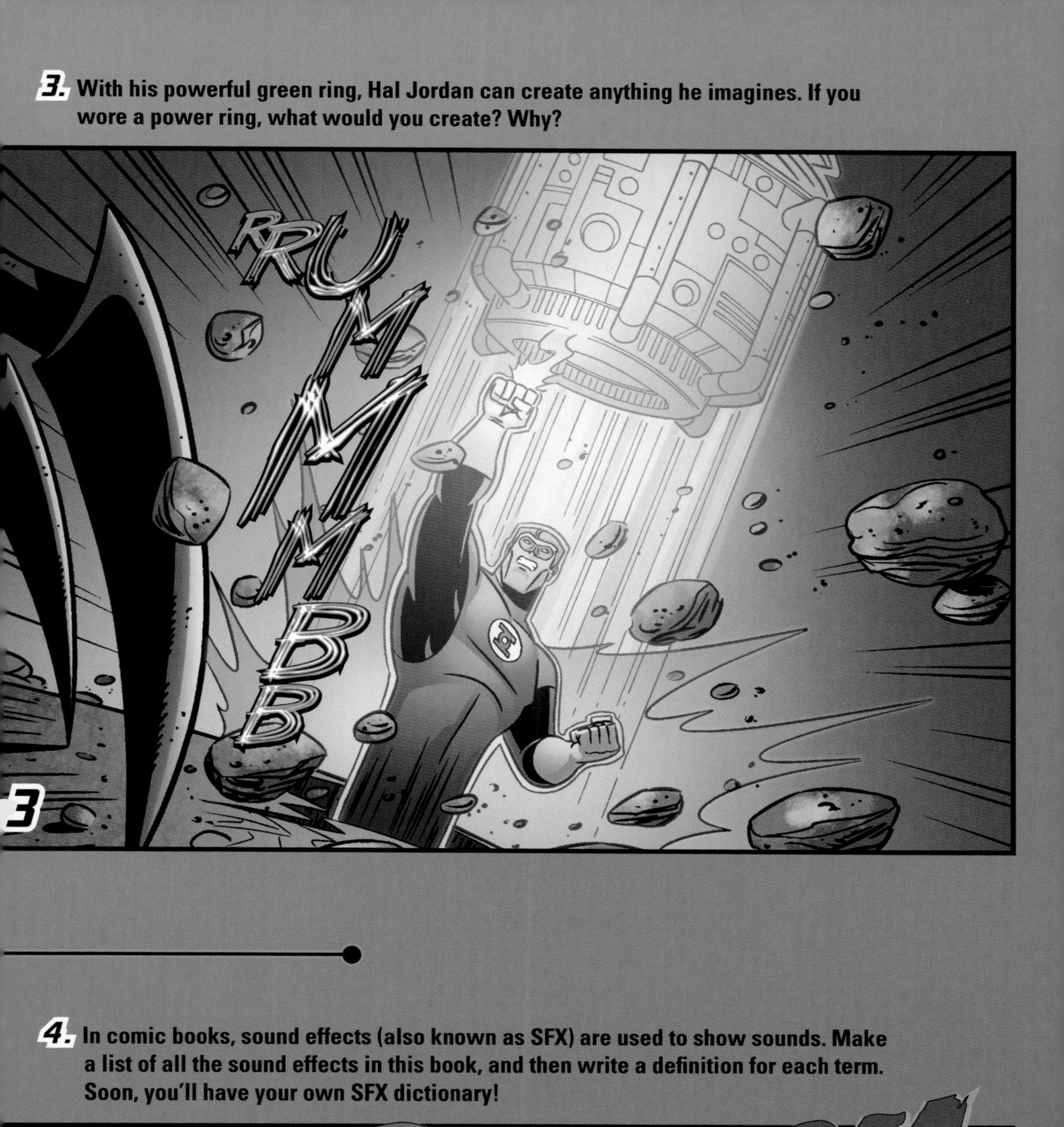
RRUMMMBB
3

4. In comic books, sound effects (also known as SFX) are used to show sounds. Make a list of all the sound effects in this book, and then write a definition for each term. Soon, you'll have your own SFX dictionary!

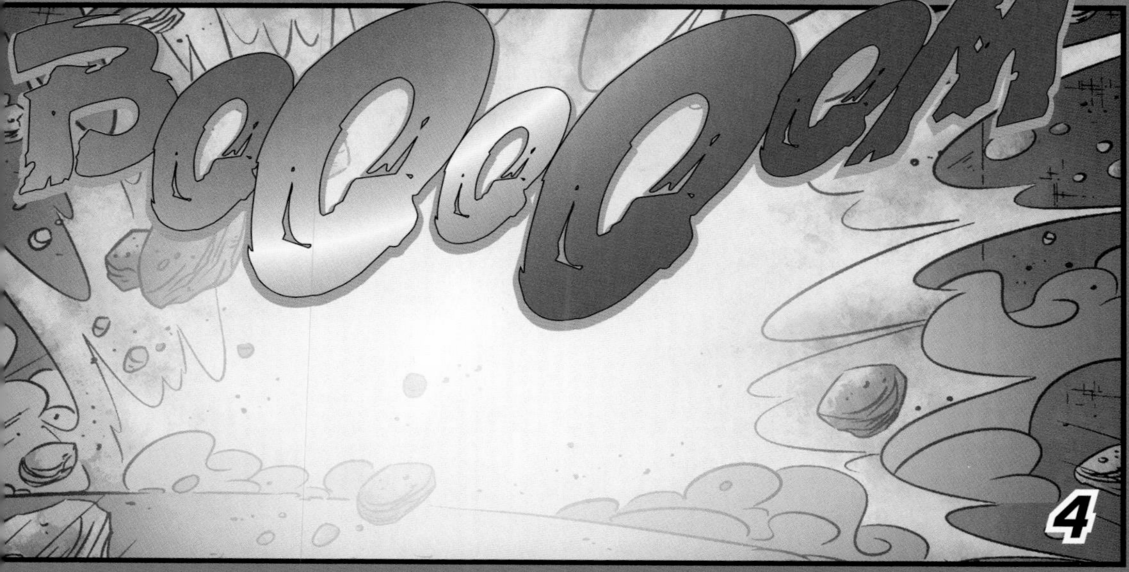
BOOOOOM
4

READ THEM ALL!

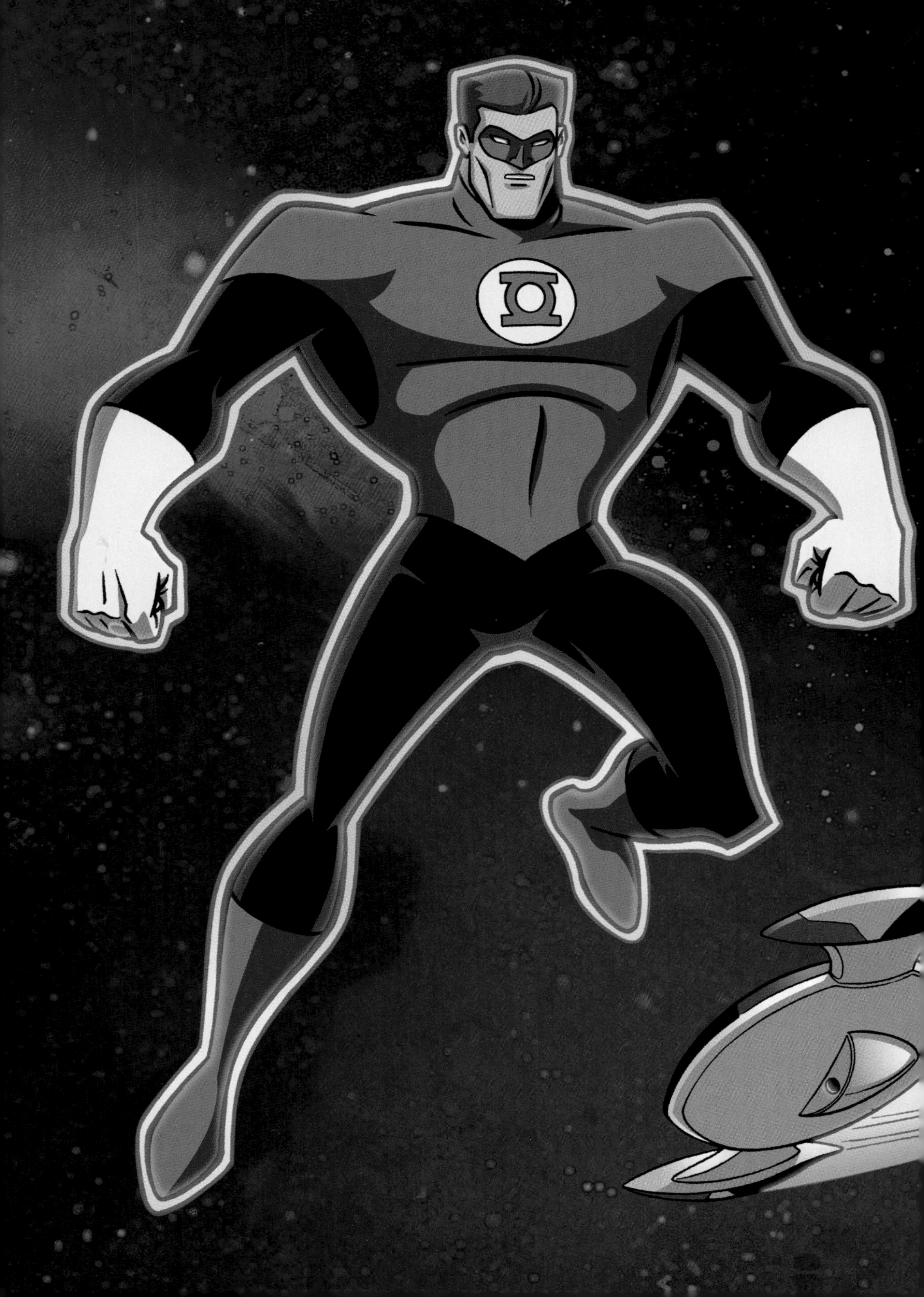

GREEN LANTERN
THE ANIMATED SERIES™
GREEN LANTERN THE ANIMATED SERIES™
TRUE COLORS
BALTAZAR • FRANCO • BRIZUELA
GREEN LANTERN THE ANIMATED SERIES™
THE INVISIBLE DESTROYER
BALTAZAR • FRANCO • BRIZUELA
GREEN LANTERN THE ANIMATED SERIES™
SNIPER!
GOT HIM!
BOUNTY HUNTER
BALTAZAR • FRANCO • BRIZUELA
GREEN LANTERN THE ANIMATED SERIES™
COUNTERFEITS
BALTAZAR • FRANCO • BRIZUELA
only from...
STONE ARCH BOOKS™
a capstone imprint www.capstonepub.com

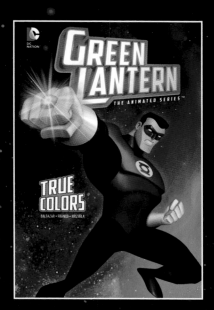

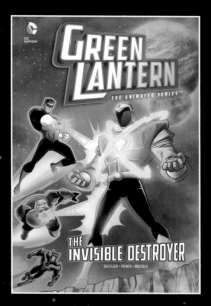

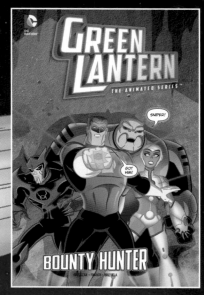

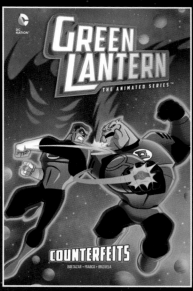

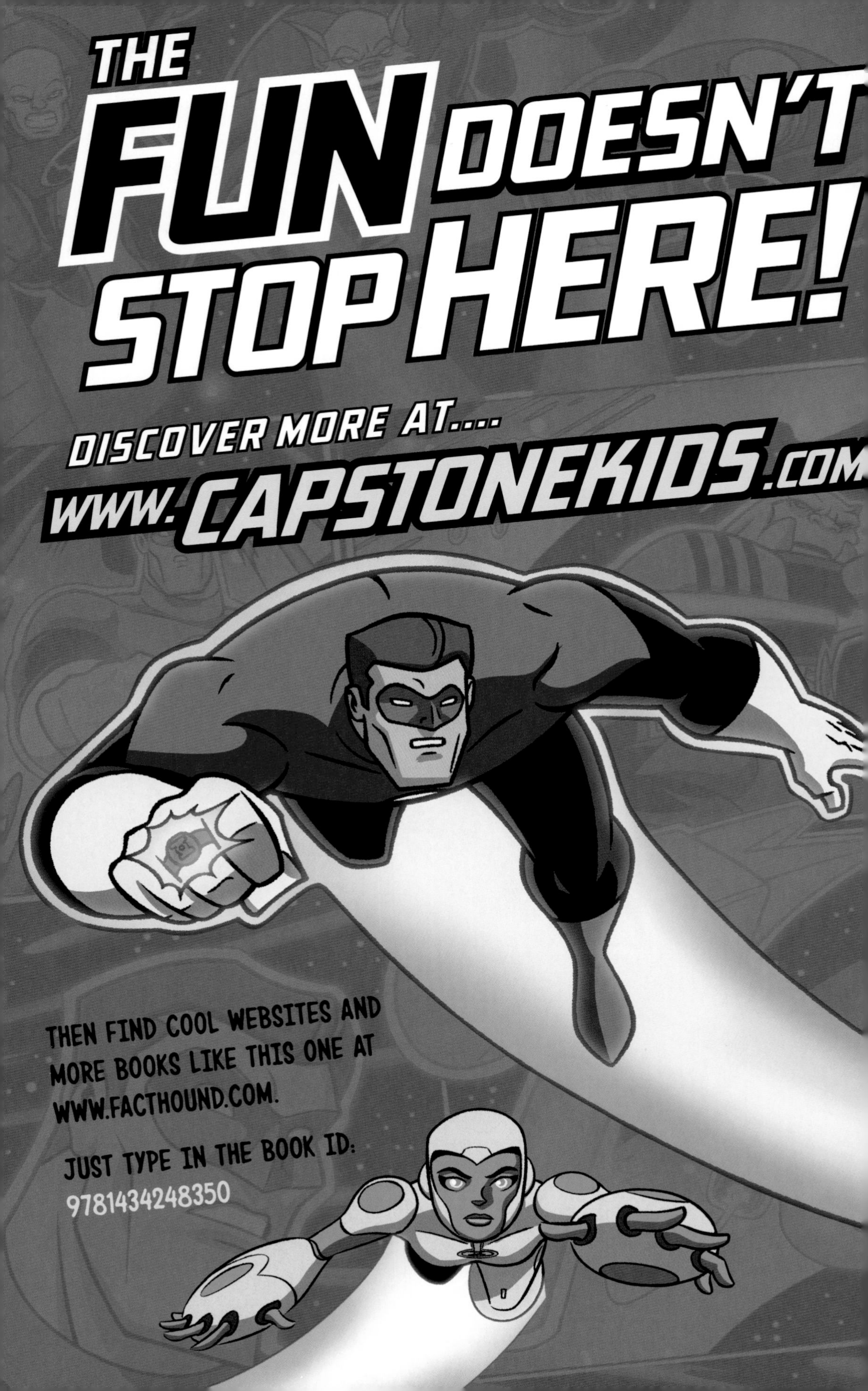
THE FUN DOESN'T STOP HERE!
DISCOVER MORE AT....
WWW.CAPSTONEKIDS.COM
THEN FIND COOL WEBSITES AND MORE BOOKS LIKE THIS ONE AT WWW.FACTHOUND.COM.
JUST TYPE IN THE BOOK ID:
9781434248350